THE TWO LIVES OF ANNIE MCGRAW

TRANSCENDING ADVERSITY

SHERRY MADDEN NEARY

ISBN 978-1-304-42459-4

Produced through Lulu.com

Dedication

To my Husband Frank
who said these stories should be written.

Table of content, page 7

DISCLAIMER

All characters in these stories and poems are fictional. Any reference to real persons real or living is coincidental. The exception may apply to brief reference to famous public figures. The general setting for these stories are likewise fictional, even though some real geographical places or names can be used.

Artwork

Artwork, with the exception of the front cover photo, is copyright protected by the artist, Joshua Seidl, SSP. It is his expressed and written pleasure that these works of art produced by him be used for this book. Page layout: Joshua Seidl. SSP

Table of Contents

FORWARD

Brother Joshua Seidl, SSP

Are children as resilient as their abusers say? Do they forget as the self-absorbed, apathetic, and beaten down spouse parent wish they would be? Or, do they become deaf, dumb and blind as in the 1969 rock opera *Tommy* by the music group, The Who? Sherry Neary's poem, *Strength in Weakness*, gives voice to pain as truth breaks through the silent barriers of domestic abuse.

"I stay the same age I was in the crib," confesses another adult in Neary's poem, *Conversation With Myself*. We all have a child within, that being our childhood. Neary touches that child. Every hand, by nature, contains salt that can sting these raw grazed hearts and other wounds. This is true even for the most delicate and caring hand reaching to heal. The momentary sting is welcomed if it is from one who can be trusted. What of those who pour salt into the wound not for any healing properties, but because they know it will hurt?

Neary speaks for those who put on the fine dresses and coats their abusive husbands bought them. One thinks of those ladies with sunglasses to veil the black eyes makeup can't cover. A stubborn wounded pride will not surrender to sound reason and positive purpose, but covers up. The little children, the unwanted mistakes, put on a strong front. Yet, they imagine themselves walking with arms crossed above the waist nursing a stomach punched by words.

We hear of that in families, in Churches and in civic organizations. We may or not be aware of who among our acquaintances are like those in these stories. I was honored when I was asked to sum things up for Neary's book. I felt it was imperative to publish these stories as much for the topics as for her excellent delivery and writing style.

Auntie Sherry, as I call the author, shared her first published work with me, *Lorraine.* It is one of the most powerful pro-life presentations I have ever read. It does not carry on as one might expect of a pro-life story, but I am certain most readers can see how it is a life topic. The issues are not limited to the moment and means that a baby leaves a womb. The ugly, shameful secrets hidden behind many doors in our communities initiate the domino effect that ends up harming or killing the innocent ones. We see how the good can be transformed to evil. These stories also show how wrong can be reformed to accomplish good. Thus, I have come to see in my own way, many reasons for Neary's subtitle for this book, *Transcending Adversity.*

In *Medicine Pouch*, Neary writes of the protagonist: Wearing a flimsy see-through purple blouse … her eyes swept the room: a predator stalking her prey.

Within, however, is a heart haunted from when someone preyed upon her as a child. She subconsciously seeks a prey that will swallow her.

These stories are provocative with a positive goal in mind. They prod the consciousness with promise to develop in positive living ways. They are not written to disparage, but rather with hope. They are written by someone who dedicated her time and career so that those who once crawled and wept, will now dance and leap and laugh from joy. They pull out soul-searching questions aimed at positive development.

"How do you explain being touched by God?"

Neary dangles possible answers in her composition in the story, *The Lesson.*

Native American story telling more often than not has abrupt, unsolved endings like we read in *Lorraine* and some other works by Neary. Lorraine's dilemma is dumped in the hearer's lap without resolve and without articulating a moral to the story. We, the readers, suddenly find ourselves holding this unfinished saga. We cannot go back and have the story re-written and sanitized. Nothing prepared any of us to hold the young daughter Maddie back and shield her eyes and ears from what just took place. Like Maddie, we can only move forward. How? Can you or I reason with Max without increasing his wrath?

Getting involved is a serious risk to ourselves and as well as to little Maddie and women in Lorraine's situation.

These stories heal. They offer hope for those groping in and from dark places. For those of us who are fortunate to have had secured upbringings, marriages and families, Neary sheds light on what some of our neighbors might be going through. There are abusive Maxes and beaten down Lorraines in all walks of life, and in every economy, race and religions. It takes the healthy and it takes those who have been there and crawled into a new light to recognize the signs and to learn the best means to intervene and break the wretched cycle of generational abuse. It is unfair to excuse the abused who becomes an abuser; but understanding the signs can lead us to the correct methods of intervention.

Prayer is powerful, but it necessitates that we do; that we act. Protesting outside abortion clinics might have saved a few. Rooting out the domestic causes of abuse is a preventative measure that will save countless more, the unborn and those unwanted, unappreciated and those born to be abused. Love is not always lacking. Rather it is twisted and distorted. Understanding the reasons does not lesson the pain. Self-righteous chastising clichés, in many cases, is in itself a link in the chain of abuse.

Neary has another unique gift in writing, and that is in her descriptive character development. I am delighted with her description of six Church ladies packed like tomatoes into a blue sedan. The Prophet and prayer brings them together to make the journey in faith, but each lady is there for her own purpose and need, because of their own unique personal histories, seeking something, someone or some answer for themselves. Their reasons are personal to each individual, yet a common faith enticed them to travel together.

Intro

She Laughs

Grasping the shadow of an eagle's wing
she flies
and while in transit she's
transformed
and soon the wingbeats become
her own as
swooping close to those she loves
she touches
with feather soft thoughts and dreams
she heals
they wake and find that they
are whole
and in the distance hear
a sound
as dropping back to earth
she laughs
and dropping back to earth
she laughs

PART 1

LORRAINE

1934

Lorraine stepped out of the shower, dried herself with a Turkish towel, wrapping herself in an ice blue satin gown. Bending forward and shaking her head, she watched as the drops flew through a shaft of sunlight to the floor. Maddie, the three year old daughter of Lorraine and her husband Max, concentrated intently as her mother prepped herself for the day

Combing gel through her black, thick hair, she then carefully formed deep undulations, clamping the high ridges. Inspection with a mother-of-pearl mirror confirmed the job to be perfect. Then, of course, came the inevitable cold cream, followed by inflating her cheeks and slapping them with the backs of her hands to ward off wrinkles. After all, you never knew when age might creep up on you. And, there could always be someone younger, more beautiful-like redheaded Marsha, the one who modeled for the painting on the WACS recruiting poster. As if she would ever go to war!

Maddie watched and mimicked every move. Lorraine called her over and sitting her on a chair, began to lovingly comb her thin, light hair, thinking hopefully that she saw a wisp of curl, but it was only a little tangle. Still, by carefully combing in gel and pinning with bobby pins and clamps, Lorraine worked at achieving a wave in her daughter's hair. This was the only child she ever wanted.

Maddie worshipped her mother, and that was what kept her mother alive. Her worship was an acknowledgement of Lorraine's overriding gift – beauty. She didn't see herself as needing to connect with other people; they should connect with her. So what if her husband ran a gas station? It was on the fashionable Miracle Mile and he had servants of the stars as his customers, and, he was high up with the union bosses.

Lorraine went to her dressing table and began to put on her make-up for the day: oil moisturizer, pancake makeup, and a cloud of powder. She applied a startlingly red lipstick to her lips then pressed them together. She carefully examined the result, turning her head several times to make sure that the fading bruise by her left eye didn't show through. After dabbing Tabu behind each ear from the bottle she had smuggled across the Tijuana border, she was ready to get dressed.

She put on a two-piece light weight suit, rather simple in style. Only the 'in' people would recognize that it came from I.Magnin: one of those special gifts from Max. Turning her attention to Maddie, she took out the hairpins and began running her fingers through scalp-warmed hair. She loved dressing and primping her little girl – the only child she would ever love. Her hands lingered over the small child's head; then she lifted up her face to give her a smile and a kiss.

Between Max, Maddie, her own personal needs, and taking care of the house, Lorraine felt it would be impossible to add another child. And yet, secretly she knew that new life was stirring in her. She didn't want it to be; Max wouldn't want another child to support.

"This is too much for me already!" She could hear him now. She had tried the old remedies, especially hot baths, but nothing happened .

There was a syrup you could buy from one of the old ladies, and that was what she was getting dressed for today. It was not for the usual stroll downtown with Maddie, looking in store windows, handling new yardage, and then having an ice cream cone before going to the market to purchase groceries for that night's dinner. Today their destination was a house at the end of a street - with a yard full of flowers and interesting plants. Stories about that kind of house usually included peeling paint and shuttered windows, but this house was a fresh white with windows open to the air.

She dressed Maddie carefully, making sure that neither her slip or underwear showed, and that her sox were in perfect alignment. They twirled together in front of the full-length mirror in the entryway, then turned to go out the front door. The sun shone brightly on them as they walked down the stone steps. A right turn on the city's sidewalk sent them facing toward Mrs. Grimaldi's house, and hopefully, relief from Lorraine's situation. She had heard of women using coat hangers, but she was afraid to do that: she knew of women who had died.

"What time is it, Mommy?" Lorraine looked down at the famous designer lapel watch, another special gift from Max.

"It's almost 10:30", she replied. A little sigh escaped her lips. Hopefully this will soon be over, she thought.

A few blocks farther and they reached Mrs. Grimaldi's front walk. Lorraine hesitated, a common occurrence witnessed from inside the house. Finally, she straightened her shoulders and bravely went up the walk. She had barely knocked when the lady of the house opened the door, smiling.

"Come in, come in, she greeted. "Sit down! Would you like a cup of tea?"

"Oh, no," Lorraine said. "We can't stay."

"I suppose I already know why you are here. You have that look. All you girls get that look. Shows right away. Have you tried anything else?

"I've tried scalding hot baths," said Lorraine, "it didn't work."

"No, that doesn't always work," replied the little old lady, ruffling her immaculate white apron. "I have something that WORKS! But you have to be certain you really want it to work, because there is no going back once you take it."

"It must work!" Lorraine knew she didn't have a choice.

Lorraine stood up as the older woman went into a back room and returned with a little unmarked bottle of dark liquid. Mrs. Grimaldi gave her a price and instructions on how to use the homemade remedy, then placed it in her hand. Lorraine looked hesitantly at the bottle in her palm, then pulled cash from her purse. She took Maddie by the hand and quickly went down the path toward home.

"What did the lady give you, mommy?"

"Nothing!" Lorraine said crossly.

Maddie sighed. She knew it was useless to question her mother further, and most of all, she should not say anything to her father. You learn many things in a family.

That night, Lorraine woke with terrible cramps and felt a warm sticky spot under her. She jumped up and went into the

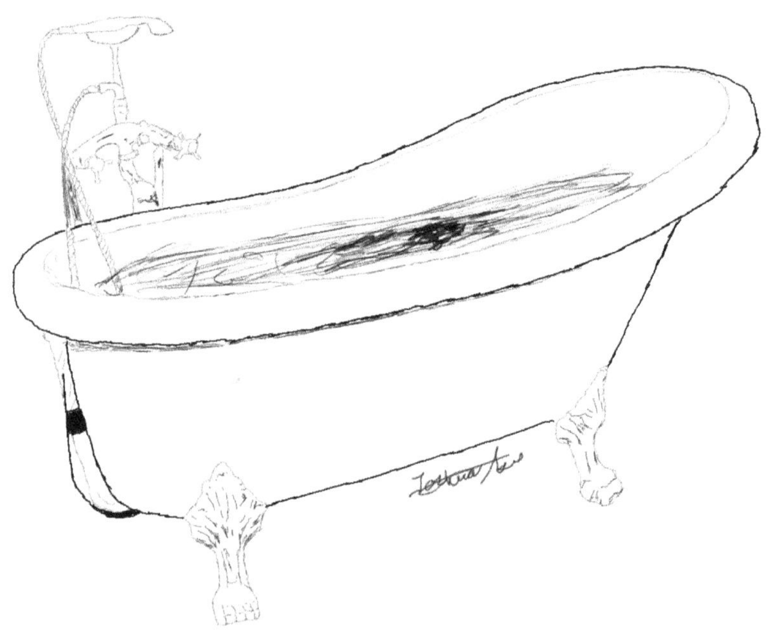

bathroom, running a small warm bath. She eased into it, not knowing what to expect. A great rush of pain, more blood, an involuntary push, and into the shallow water swooshed a small object. It was a perfect little baby. As she picked it up. It let out a tiny cry. Just one. Then it went lifeless.

Max heard her get up, and was coming into the bathroom just in time to hear the cry.

"What have you done?" He grabbed her out of the tub and began punching her in the face and in her stomach. She didn't reply, and he didn't stop for a very long time.

The next night Max came home with a big package – another one of his special presents. There was a long red hair on his jacket.

Lorainne never forgot the sound of that little cry, and years later Maddie heard her mother cry out in the night:

"What have I done?"

The Bremerton Ferry

1940

It seemed such a short time since she had ridden with Nana and Granddad down the buttercup strewn highway. That had been in an afternoon. This time it was night, and snow was piled where the buttercups grew, and Annie was wrapped in one of Nana's quilts. She watched her breath escaping in steamy puffs, making clouds on the windows of the old Chevy. "They're good cars, but they're a bugger to start", Granddad would say every time he put the key into the ignition; turning the key until the engine groaned and finally came to life. It took longer, and more groans tonight. The air was cold, below freezing. More than once along the way, Nana reminded her that as much as she had enjoyed Christmas there was one more big surprise in store for her. She couldn't believe anything would be better.

Granddad carried the 5 year old into the house through the back porch and kitchen, putting her down in a rocking chair next to the pot bellied stove in the living room. She watched in fascination as he stoked the fire into flame at the dancing, sputtering sparks. The cold linoleum floor crackled as he shifted his weight, adding logs from the nearby basket of logs and kindling. It was the only source of heat, except for the kitchen's cast iron stove.

The warmth made Annie sleepy, and as she drifted off, she relived the wonderful Christmas she had just experienced, first in memory, then in dream. She didn't recall that there were presents, but surely there were. She just remembered taking the Bremerton Ferry across the bay to Uncle Ray's. He was working in the shipyards. Whispers between adults talked of rumors of war. It sounded serious, something little children shouldn't know about.

Had Annie known how to spell, she would have renamed the beautiful ship the Bremerton Fairy. All the way to Seattle, she glowed with excitement. Her first glimpse of the ferry exceeded her expectations. It was long and sleek, bright lights shining from myriad openings in the decks of the magic white ship. Each opening gave a view to the passengers of the water churning from the bow, and a glimpse, even at night, of the towering snow capped mountains that overlooked their destination. Annie's dad, Max, held her up so she could see. Her delight brought a smile to his often cruel lips.

Arriving very late at Uncle Ray's, all the rest of the family was asleep. Cousins were crowded onto the floor, covered in blankets, huddled close for warmth. Lorraine, Annie's mother, insisted that the fragile little girl had to sleep with her and Max in the bed reserved for them. Annie started to cry. Just once, even though they were asleep, she wanted to be with her cousins. Along with her sister Maddie, they always went off without her.

Finally, Max and Granddad convinced Lorraine to let Annie sleep with the others. Bundled up in a blanket, they placed her in the middle of that august company. She was awake until dawn, listening to the breathing, feeling the blankets pulled this way and that, feeling closer to her cousins than she ever would again. She knew, even at that tender age, that these were moments to be treasured, never to be forgotten or repeated.

By tradition, no one – that is children - were allowed to get up until Granddad called out "Merry Christmas", his eyes twinkling and a rare broad smile emerged on his face. His family, as plain people, never celebrated Christmas. So it was a particularly happy occasion for his little rebellion. Nana's family's religious beliefs denied 'feast days', so Christmas was a celebration of family, rather than the birth of Jesus.

In her dream, the smells of bacon mingled with the aroma of turkey, dressing, and Nana's fresh apple pies. As she came to the brink of consciousness, Granddad was carrying her to the bedroom. Nana had taken two oak chairs from the kitchen and placed them side by side, pushing seats toward their bed, with an old maple chair placed at the end away from the head of the bed, forming a crib. She then piled a couple of carefully folded comforters on the seats for a mattress.

"You will be warm and you won't fall out. You'll be right next to me if you need anything."

Then right before Granddad laid Annie down, Nana reminded her of the big surprise. She kissed her on the forehead and whispered the words her granddaughter loved to hear: "My little sweet heart and candy bones." Annie drifted off to sleep again, thinking of how much she loved going to be with Nana and Granddad.

Facing the highway, the house had been the original home of the apple orchard owner. Now, it was the residence of the orchard superintendent. Granddad's Quaker family had a history of being orchardists back to Scotland in the 1600's. Whatever tree Granddad planted or cared for thrived. Granddad was tall and straight. His clear blue eyes paired with the little smirk at the corner of his lips, always appeared ready to break into a smile.

Nana had dark wavy hair that she always had cut at the barber shop – not too short! - it was foolishness to pay beauty parlor prices. "Waste not, want not", was her motto. She seemed to always be wearing an apron: for cooking, cleaning, and gathering vegetables. Sometimes she let Annie sort tiny pieces of fabric for quilts into egg carton squares as she cut them.

It was the middle of the night when the bedroom light went on and Nana gently nudged Annie awake.

"The surprise is here!"

Annie rubbed her eyes, anxious to see 'the surprise'. But it was just Uncle Ray and his girlfriend, Lucille. She was confused. This was the same couple who took her for rides in Uncle Ray's shiny black Chevy convertible, hair flying and laughing for joy. The same couple who gave her a rabbit's fur scarf and muffler 'just because they loved her'. The uncle with the dark skin, wavy black hair and stunning blue eyes. And her Lucille, the red haired nurse with crinkley eyes and broad smile.

Seeing Annie's dismay, Nana said brightly "They just got married! Now she is your *Aunt* Lucille!"

It still didn't make sense to the little girl. What was changed? Wasn't she going to still be her friend? This didn't seem like such a good thing to her. It got worse.

"We are moving to California', Uncle Ray said, as if that was something really special.

Annie just wanted to go back to sleep and pretend everything was the way it had been. The way it was supposed to be. So this was why she had come home with her grandparent's – for the 'big surprise'. But then, she was used to disappointment. This would be OK in time. Even at that tender age, children know how to cope.

Annie was unusually quiet for a few days. Her dad brought home Mike, a terrier that never left her side. He was often seen leaning against her in family photos. She let Mike fill the hole left by her two special people. Eventually, Annie and her family all moved to California near each other. Annie had heart surgery there, but it was unsuccessful, leaving her with the same weakened heart and lungs, and susceptible to pneumonia. Uncle Ray and 'Aunt' Lucille came every month. He hung around with his sister, Annie's mother, while Lucille held syringes of penicillin in beeswax to soften them enough to inject – a World War II adaptation for soldiers in the field. She would hold them for an hour or so and visit with Annie. The injections were painful, but being with her aunt made it bearable, and helped keep her from getting sick.

After Annie was grown and had children of her own, Lucille would give them penicillin shots when they got sick, coming to Annie's house to administer them. When Lucille was dying of cancer, Annie, who had moved far away with her family, flew to be with her toward the end. She could still smile that broad smile, and her eyes almost twinkled. And they talked of those long ago days of driving around in the convertible, of cracker jacks at ball games, and the Christmas they rode the Bremerton Ferry.

All Aboard!

1944

It was one of those incredibly clear bright early summer days in Southern California that were so plentiful in the '40's. There was a light breeze off the ocean, and Annie was on her way to her Nana's. Her mother Lorraine dropped Annie off at the bus stop that would take her down Glenoaks Boulevard, through Glendale, then to downtown Los Angeles. There she would transfer to the red car going south toward Artesia. Her final stop would be the one right before Artesia, where Nana would meet her. The idea of making this adventurous trip all by herself was exhilarating, making her tingle all over. Annie, wearing her first pair of patent leather shoes and sox that matched the light blue dress she wore, was fairly dancing with excitement.

The bus trip was uneventful, but, when the bus reached downtown Los Angeles, where the smells of foods of many nationalities mingled with the stench of poverty and the perfumes of the rich, her heart started racing and Annie could barely breathe. It was exciting to see all the colors, not only of skins but of fabrics, flowers, and window displays. Annie imagined walking those streets, mingling with the crowds, looking in the windows, and listening to the street preachers in Pershing Square.

It was in this panoply of humanity that she made a connection with the big red streetcar that would take her to Nana's. Blocks before it reached the corner where she boarded, the clacking of the wheels and the clanging of the bells echoed off the buildings, announcing its impending arrival. As it neared, every once in awhile the car hit a bump in the tracks and sparks would fly from the little wheel that connected to the power source: two electric cables that were strung down the middle of the street, one for each direction. Passengers waited on the corner, peering first toward the approaching coach, then toward the stoplight and the traffic. It was important to be ready to run for the marked off area next to the tracks in the middle of the street without being hit by oncoming traffic. As the red car came rocking, those waiting on the corner ran to the passenger area. Annie climbed up the tall steps, watching and listening as the fare coins swirled noisily down the rectangular glass receiver. The folding doors swung closed at the circular turn of the handle by the conductor, and they were on their way. Annie didn't want to miss any part of this trip.

Staggering to the middle of the car, Annie nearly fell into a seat as the wheels engaged, swaying the car as it gathered momentum. She slid across the shiny wood slat seat to the window, which to her delight, was open. The conductor frequently rang the bell to alert the cars that shared the roadway, and to let possible passengers know it was on its way. The car bounced over a track connection, and they were no longer on the city streets but traveling along the same tracks as the trains. The car passed Olvera Street: its burrito, taco, enchilada and menudo stands sent waves of delicious odors into the air. Colorfully dressed women with sweet little hands patted tortillas behind windows, alternating the dough from palm to palm getting larger and larger until the flat rounds were ready to be grilled on huge flat topped stoves. Brilliant piñatas in animal shapes hung from corners of the food stand awnings. Mariachi bands strolled through the open air market, guitars and voices recalling the old songs from Mexico.

They passed Union Station: the graceful Spanish style building flanked by palm trees and its white plaster walls topped by the red tiles which personified Los Angeles. A steady stream of people entered this terminus of transportation, which united the southland with the rest of the country. Newspapers often carried photos of famous politicians and movie stars as they boarded or detrained, the women flashing teeth and diamonds, furs hanging from their shoulders, men in their expensive suits and natty ties. Across the street, under ancient trees with low hanging branches was the little Franciscan church which in earlier times held services for the original inhabitants, but now only occasionally, serving the dwindling population of faithful Hispanics

Her head twisted from side to side to take in the sights, sounds and aromas of this wonderful place. They passed Felipe's, which served the best pastrami sandwiches and the hottest mustard in the world. Annie remembered getting to take a pickled, red died egg from a jar on the counter, and the sawdust on the wooden floor on an excursion with her parents. Long tables with benches invited customers to sit, while others waited at the deli style counters for their French roll encased pastrami sandwiches. Across the street, policemen were gently prodding awake vagrants who had slept in the doorway of an abandoned building, unnoticed by men from City Hall with their Brooks Brothers suits and their alligator briefcases. They passed the tall isolated white building next to the railroad tracks that had a huge faded black 'Henry's Spaghetti' on its dreary side, and started on their way in earnest.

Encampments of homeless, with their cardboard houses and shopping cart closets along the metal fence, was a reminder that not everything in this world is wonderful. This sad scene was rapidly replaced by tidy neighborhoods of small white clapboard homes with metal barred windows. Picket fences surrounded the yards where only a few blades of grass valiantly grew. Odors of chicken mole' with its exotic combination of seasonings wafted in the air. Gracefully executed graffiti adorned sides of garages. As the car swayed, the sounds of children playing, with rumblings of Chevy's mufflers turned into a song of humanity. Gradually the Latino neighborhood merged into South Central.

If there was gang activity, it was not apparent to her. There were no Crips or Bloods in those days. Riots had not yet broken out because of the oppressive practice of sending the better meat and produce to the affluent neighborhoods and the leftovers to the Black community, which was virtually landlocked and captive to the available stores run by unscrupulous store owners charging exorbitant prices. Fires had not yet been set on couches put together with cardboard and staples then sold as fine furniture. But she didn't know about such things when she was in the fifth grade-going-on-sixth. All she saw was a variety of humanity, which she found truly beautiful: rich dark brown skin with black hair and homes painted vibrant purples, greens and blues.

Southbound toward Bellflower, home of the Dutch dairies, were neighborhoods where children mostly had blond hair, blue eyes, and pale skin. The homes all had carefully manicured lawns, sedately painted white with dark trim, giving it an overly proper look, as if to distract from the oppressive animal odors. The air which had carried such an exuberant variety of smells and sounds was drowned out by the mooing of cows and stench of their waste making her nose twitch and her asthmatic lungs start wheezing. That smell signaled that the end of her trip was near. Nana and Granddad lived just beyond the reach of that stink. They came into an area where large vegetation was growing along the track, making it feel like they were out in the country. The air was heating up, the red car was rocking, and she was getting hungry. The car slowed and the conductor called out her stop:

"Norwalk, Norwalk Boulevard! All passengers going to Norwalk or Artesia prepare to detrain."

Annie carefully climbed down the steps, having to jump from the last step and nearly falling. There, standing alongside the railroad track, was her Nana. Once a tall woman, she had a slight hump on her shoulders, the result of a fall down a stone cellar stairway as a young girl. She wore black orthopedic shoes with a simple cotton dress that had little pink and lavender flowers on it. Her short wavy hair glistened in the sun. Nana met her with a kiss on the top of her head as she whispered "Sweet Heart and Candy Bones". Nana seldom smiled with her lips, but her piercing black eyes did it for her, mellowing and with tears pooling. She took Annie's little suitcase, and they walked the short distance to the house that she and Granddad rented. Granddad was away picking peaches in an orchard, so it would be just the two of them. Her grandparents never owned a home, and moved frequently as jobs became available. Granddad had lost his job as manager of an orange grove to a young man who married his employer's daughter. Many of the orchards were being leveled to build homes for the newly burgeoning population of the Southland. Aircraft factories were replacing agriculture as the economic base, leaving men like Granddad with little hope for permanent employment.

And so, Annie settled in for a quiet week. Annie loved that Nana never treated her as a sickly child, even though she had been since birth. Nana had a vast knowledge of many subjects, and always kept up with the latest news, about which she had distinct and often vocal views. She frequented the local library, bringing home books which were marked 'removed from library'. She had gone to pick up a few books in preparation for Annie's visit: Spring Came on Forever by Bess Streeter Aldrich and The Robe by Lloyd C. Douglas. They were her first 'grown up' books. Annie found The Robe inspiring and exciting and created a desire to know more about historic people and times. Spring Came on Forever made her cry, and wonder about the injustices of life. The circumstances and the landscapes were far too bleak for her young mind. She thought that it disappointed Nana, since she, too, had grown up on the prairie and had known its hardships. It no doubt helped to form her grandmother into the strong, independent woman she was.

One day, Nana told Annie to comb her hair and wash her face, (which she had done earlier), and put on a clean dress. It wasn't Sunday, so she knew they weren't going to church. She wasn't one you wanted to question, so Annie simply did what she was told.

"We have to go to the feed store", Nana announced.

"The feed store?" Annie thought. They didn't live on the ranch anymore.

Nana made her preparations, even face powder, rouge and lipstick. Annie marveled at how she dabbed on the lipstick, tightly pursing her lips together then making a little circle of red. Surprisingly, Nana's lipstick usually looked quite good. Then she put on a 'Sunday-go-to-meeting' hat, as she always did when going 'out'. Without question, Annie followed her out the door, and they started walking down the cracked sidewalk toward the tiny shopping area several blocks away. 'Feed store' was apparently Nana's generic name for any store.

They went into a shop with high, green faded tongue and groove walls and a wooden floor which had felt the footsteps of generations. Straight ahead was a soda fountain with high stools. A brass foot rail aided Annie's climb to the seat. It had a linoleum counter top - a marble design in shades of blue. It had been a hot dusty walk, but a huge ceiling fan kept the dim shop pleasantly cool. She knew this was going to be big occasion. She had never heard of Nana doing anything as extravagant as spending money in a coffee shop.

She asked Annie "Have you ever had a chocolate ice cream soda?"

To which Annie replied "No, I haven't."

"Well, we are going to have one." she announced

Nana nodded to the woman behind the counter, who got out two tall spiral-designed glasses that were frosted cold. She took a scoop of vanilla ice cream and plopped one into each glass. Then she poured some chocolate syrup into each one, and a squirt of soda water and another scoop of ice cream, after which she put the glasses onto the machine that mixed milkshakes. She repeated the process, giving one to each of them, with a long spoon, a napkin, and a straw. Annie had never tasted anything so excruciatingly delicious. It was nearly impossible to get her to eat anything but crisp bacon and a glass of milk.

"I believe I could live on this marvelous concoction!"

Nana smiled one of her rare smiles and gave her a little hug, whether because of her response, or the use of her burgeoning vocabulary.

A couple of days later, on Saturday, Nana again told her to wash her hands and face, comb her hair and put on a fresh dress. She wondered what kind of adventure she had for her this time. She hoped it would be another soda, but they walked on passed the soda fountain. They went to the next block, then to the one after that, to where the movie theatre was. That couldn't be where they were going! Nana didn't approve of movies, and doctors had told Mother that she couldn't go to the movies for fear she would get too excited and go into heart failure. Would Nana really risk going against her values, going against doctor's orders – and spend money foolishly? *All on the same day?*

Apparently she would do all three, because they stopped at the end of the line leading to the cashier's booth.

"It's a matinee" she said looking down at her with a wise expression. "It will only cost five cents for me, and you are free, being under 12".

So they waited in line to see Gene Autrey in one of his many 'singing cowboy' movies. It was a good movie, mainly because it was Annie's first, and because she was with her Nana. Annie didn't go into heart failure.

The next day, Sunday, they went to church. Nana's strong alto voice harmonized with the sopranos and baritones singing the old Southern gospel songs. There was a bit of a twang in the a capella voices. Annie, fascinated by the shiny diamond pattern on the back of Nana's hands and the flies that flew around in the dense hot air served the purpose of keeping Annie awake. The preacher reminded them that they are all sinners in a loud voice and quoted chapter and verse to prove it. At the end of his sermon, the preacher went to the plain table in the front of the church and presented a stack of round wooden trays with little holes that held tiny goblets of red grape juice. Beside it, he placed a pile of flat silver plates with rounds of unleavened, lightly baked and scored bread.

He proclaimed: "This is not the blood of Christ; this is not the body of Christ. It is for a remembrance only". The trays and plates of not body and not blood were passed around for everyone who was baptized to share. Then the baskets on long poles came around so that donations could be made to support the congregation while they sang 'Amazing Grace'.

Then the preacher asked if there was anyone who wanted to be baptized and give their life to Jesus. Everyone sang 'Just As I Am' while the preacher, hands folded under his chin and eyes closed, prayed and quietly invited anyone who wanted to confess their sins and be baptized should come forward. Toward the end of the last verse a young woman attired in a simple pink dress made her way to the front. Preacher Jones had her sit in the front row and talked to her softly. Then so we all could hear:

"Do you confess you are a sinner?" The shy lady answered "Yes."

"Do you repent of your sins?" she nodded her head in affirmation. The preacher bent down and quietly told her she needed to say it so that the people could hear.

"I do." she said firmly.

"Do you believe that Jesus was crucified, died and was buried and raised again on the third day?"

"Yes", she answered, loud enough to be heard by all.

"Do you want to be baptized?"

"Yes!"

While everyone sang "Just as I Am", the woman was taken

behind the pulpit to a back room. Soon the crimson velvet curtains in back of the pulpit and table opened as in the movie theater to expose a blue tile-sided pool. The preacher waited as the woman appeared from the side in a white full length cotton gown. He led her down into waist high water, put a kerchiefed hand over her nose and laid her into the water, baptizing her "In the name of the Father, the Son, and the Holy Ghost. Amen." She came up out of the water transformed: a smile on her face, her hair slicked back, and standing tall.

By the time the last hymn was sung, Annie was full of the many new experiences she had in the short week she was away from home. Annie just wanted to be still and absorb it all. They went to lunch with relatives: chicken pot pies in thick white bowls with flaky crust on top. She absentmindedly ate most of hers, lost in thought, and sated with many memories. She would have liked to take the red car home, but her mother came that afternoon to get her.

After a quick smile and hug she asked Annie,

"Well, what did you do?"

Nana and Annie exchanged a conspiratorial smile. "Not much."

Maddie

1948

It was an especially beautiful Southern California summer evening, made even more wonderful because Maddie was going out with Kenneth. She had met Kenneth at the beach. They had talked of many things and found they had similar interests: Tommy Dorsey's orchestra, Marilyn Monroe movies, and Frank Sinatra's soothing ballads. When Kenneth discovered they lived in adjoining towns, he asked Maddie to go with him to the new Marilyn movie. Maddie had never dated a college man before. She accepted with gusto, forgetting that she was to always ask her parents before making plans with new people.

Maddie's job at May Company in the women's department gave her access to the latest fashions. She often came home from the downtown Los Angeles store describing the beautiful clothes she had sold to prosperous customers. The latest fad was linen suits for casual wear, and floor length silk florals with peek-a-boo midriff exposed gowns for formal wear. Maddie often sewed her own clothes to keep up with her friends. But not this time. She had spent her entire month's paycheck on a grey linen suit for her date with Kenneth.

Maddie pressed and laid out the new suit with her freshly laundered bra, panties, slip, garter belt and nylon hose. Before taking her bath and shampooing her hair, Maddie used an oatmeal scrub on her face that made her skin glow. Lorraine, Maddie's mother, offered her face cream, which Maddie sparingly smoothed over

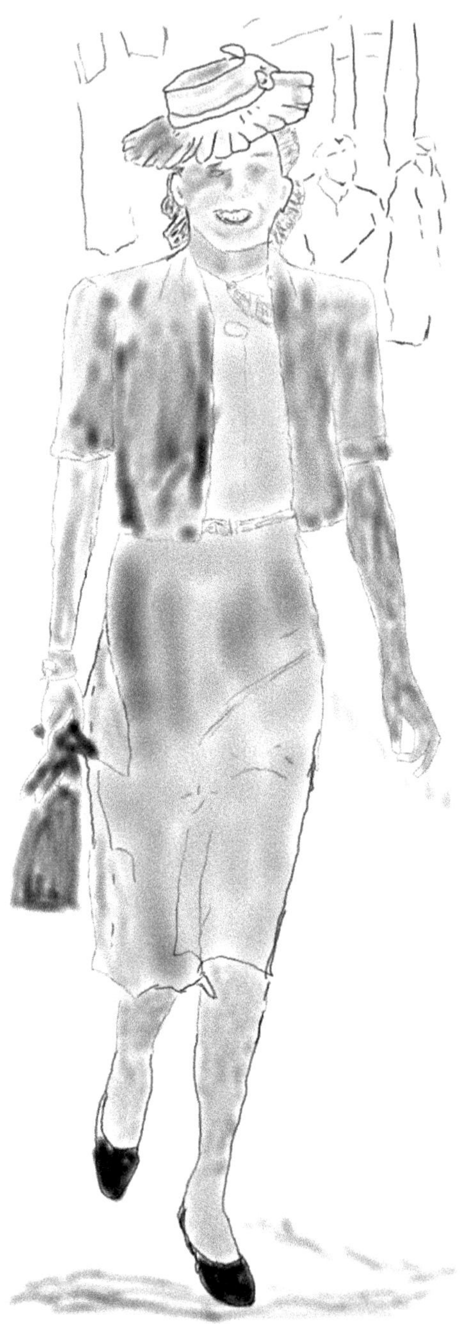

her face and neck. This routine had to be done early in the day so that her hair would be perfectly dry, ready to work into the latest coif.

Maddie was 17, going into her senior year. The only boy she had dated was Carl, who was in many of her classes. He was tall with dark wavy hair and fair skin. Except for a space between his front teeth, he was quite nice looking. He was the youngest son of a widowed mother, and they lived very modestly. This was in contrast to Kenneth, who lived in a nearby upscale community with his attorney father and socialite mother. Lorraine was beside herself thinking that finally, her daughter was dating someone worthwhile.

Around four o'clock, with her hair completely dry, Maddie put on her sundry underclothing and began working on her soft, light brown hair. Lorraine had whipped egg whites light to use on the French role Maddie wanted for her hair. All the models and movie stars, except Marilyn, were wearing their hair that way, slicked back at the sides and formed into a smooth roll from the nape of the neck to the crown of the head. It was a very sophisticated look. Between the two women, they were able to make Maddie's hair stay in that configuration with the aid of the egg whites, which when dry, held it all together. Once her hair was completely dry, she carefully dressed, making sure not to disturb her hairdo. Pulling on the nylon stockings and securing them to the garter belt was the most difficult process because she was trembling with excitement. She felt the cool silk slip slither down her body over her other undergarments, beginning to feel as sophisticated as she felt she looked. A dab of Lorraine's contraband Tabu behind each ear, and Maddie was ready to take a long appreciative look in the mirror of Lorraine's waterfall walnut dressing table.

While Maddie dressed, Lorraine began fixing dinner. Annie, Maddie's little sister, set the table for four: Lorraine, Maddie, Annie, and their young brother Jack. She didn't set a place for her dad, Max, since he rarely came home from work in time for dinner. Lorraine had prepared mashed potatoes, peas and fried round steaks, a favorite of everyone but Annie, who found the meat hard to chew, much less swallow.

Lorraine and the two younger children sat down to eat, waiting for Maddie to finish dressing. They were sipping on iced tea when Max came in the driveway blowing the wolf whistle he had installed in his car. The automatic response to their father's arrival was instant fear. His temper was totally unpredictable. They never knew when he came in whether he was going to kiss them or give them a slap. Lorraine quickly set another place for him at the table, finishing before he saw that he had not been included. No one spoke as he came in the door. They relaxed when they saw that he was in one of his good moods, full of smiles and silly jokes.

Max was hungry, so he insisted on eating immediately. He didn't seem to notice that Maddie wasn't at the table until she came in the kitchen, looking like someone on a magazine cover. Everyone except Max made comments about how lovely she looked. Max asked sarcastically where she thought she was going.

She said "On a date".

He continued eating, and everyone silently breathed a sigh of relief. After a few bites, he looked up again at Maddie and demanded to know where she was going and who with.

Annie knew that tone of voice. She looked away to not see the pink rising up her father's neck, knowing his face would look as if it was swelling and his eyes turning threateningly green. Annie started counting the dark spots left from when in a rage, he shook a bottle of Coke and let it spay all over Lorraine and the ceiling.

He seemed to settle down as Lorraine told him about Kenneth, carefully leaving out where Maddie had met him and that she hadn't asked permission. A few minutes passed and the tension seemed to ease and everyone ate as if all was normal. Max said, "Please pass the peas." Annie passed the bowl to Max. They were canned peas, and Lorraine had not drained off the juice. Because everyone liked peas, she had warmed two cans, filling a good sized bowl.

Without warning, Max stood up with the bowl and turned it upside down on Maddie's head. "Now see who wants to go out with you!" Max yelled with a smirk on his lips.

No one dared to breathe, not knowing what do expect next. Maddie sat still, stunned. Peas and juice ran down her hair and onto her new suit. Her hair, which had been so carefully set with egg whites started to sag, as did the linen of her suit. She was paralyzed with disbelief at what had just happened. One moment she was anxiously waiting to go out with Kenneth, glowing with happiness. The next moment all of her preparations were destroyed; her expectations of the evening slipping away like the peas slipping down her face, landing on her quivering lips.

No one moved. They all sat in silence except Jack, who stifled a six year old's giggle. Max stormed out of the kitchen, but the other's remained still until the doorbell rang. Maddie ran crying to her room. "I can't let him see me like this!" she sobbed. "Tell him I'm sick and can't go."

Annie was chosen to be the messenger. She opened the door to Kenneth. He had a broad smile that showed even white teeth when he asked for Maddie. Annie was so impressed with his appearance she didn't speak for a moment. He was dressed in a light blue tweed jacket with a white dress shirt and brown slacks with a knife sharp crease. He had light brown hair that was no darker than his deep tan. His blue eyes crinkled at the corners when he asked again to see Maddie. Reluctantly, Annie told him that Maddie was sick in bed and couldn't go with him. She wanted to scream that it was her father's fault, he had ruined Maddie's evening. She wanted to tell him what had happened, that he should come another time, when Max wasn't home.

Max called from the other room. "Is that jerk still here?" Kenneth's smile faded, and he turned silently away. He got into his car and drove slowly away, looking back just for an instant. Maddie cried herself to sleep. She never wore the suit again.

AWAKENING

1948

Lorraine loved to shop. It was a beautiful fall morning, and her three children were all off to school - the youngest, Jack, had just entered kindergarten. Her spirits lifted as she thought of getting out of her apron and house dress. She would wear one of her nicer outfits, the lavender suit that she wore to church. It hung a little loose on her since she had lost weight, but at least Max couldn't criticize her for being fat, which she never was.

She got out her suit and fresh underwear, laid them across the bed and headed for the shower. She put on a shower cap over her newly dyed hair - a few white strands had appeared – making sure to cover the back of her head and the bobby pinned curls.

As the warm water hit her body, she felt a little weak. Nothing to worry about, she thought. It's just the stress of dealing with building a new house, living in this dumpy place with rocks for a lawn, scorpions trying to come in, and black widow spiders in the bathtub. All that, Max's tirades, raging teen hormones, a sickly daughter and a wild five-year-old. She swept aside thoughts of Marsha, Max's lover. She would feel better once she got on the bus and headed for town.

Lorraine dried herself off with a worn towel. All of their good belongings were in storage until their new house was built. She slipped into her clothes, ignoring two little grease spots on her skirt. She removed the bobby pins and ran a brush through her still lush dark hair. Putting on her makeup, she noticed that she looked a little peaked. Oh, well, a little more rouge will cover that, she thought.

Putting on her watch, she realized she had taken more time to get ready than she thought. She changed purses to match her outfit, quickly making sure she had everything she would need: change for the bus meter; the check book; the hidden stash of money she always kept in case of a sale; and identification. A quick dab of perfume behind each earringed ear, and she was good to go.

She took off down the street, careful not to slip on the loose little rocks that constantly rolled on to the asphalt from the banks along the steep roadway. It was hard to hurry, but she didn't want to miss the bus. The bus to beautiful goods and temporary freedom! She could feel the burdens of motherhood lift from her with every step.

Lorraine crossed the busy boulevard at the stoplight and reached the bus stop just minutes before it arrived. The bus stopped, making the whoosh of compressed air as the door opened. She stepped quickly up the steps, the door folding close behind her. The bus jerked forward as her coins noisily swirled in the Keene coin box, down and out of sight. She sat down by the window in a seat toward the rear of the bus. She wanted to be alone to savor the beauty of the day and take in the immaculately landscaped homes along the way. She sighed, wishing she could live in one of the beautiful shake roofed houses where everyone was happy.

Twenty minutes later, Lorraine stepped off the bus in downtown Glendale. The sun had come out from behind the clouds, and suddenly she felt very warm. She felt herself falling to the sidewalk, but was unable to break the fall. Everything went blank. Passersby saw what was happening to Lorraine, gawking as she fell sprawling to the cement. Most just looked and walked away, but one man stopped and checked her pulse and forehead. She just seemed to have feinted, but he knew he wouldn't want his wife to be just left on a walkway in the middle of a city. He picked up her purse and found her wallet. Max's name was on some of her ID, and searching through some of the papers found a receipt that showed him to be the operator of a service station. The man went to a phone booth and looked up the phone number for the business.

The phone rang a number of times before a deep voiced woman answered. He asked for Max, waiting for several minutes before a voice cheerfully answered.

"Texaco. Max speaking. How can I help you?"

The man who found Lorraine told Max what had happened, and he thought Max would want to come take care of her. He said he would wait until Max got there.

"What has that worthless broad got to complain about now?" he fumed to himself. Max, anger rising in his voice, gruffly asked "Where is she?"

The good Samaritan was shocked at Max's response, but politely gave the location.

"I'll be there when I can get there" Max said, slamming down the receiver.

"Where's Mother?" demanded Jack, the kindergartner, as his sister Annie came through the door. "I have been home for a long time, but she isn't here! And I'm hungry!" he said indignantly.

Annie didn't know what to think of this pronouncement. Mother was always home when they came in from school. It worried her. There wasn't even a note.

"What do you want to eat," she asked. She was thinking more of what might have transpired with her mother.

"Peanut butter and jelly!" Jack chirpped.

Annie went to the institutional green cupboard that held the jars of Skippy and grape jelly. Setting them on the counter next to the bread box, she took out the half-full loaf of Wonder Bread. Every move in slow motion, the 12-year-olds' concentration was on the mounting anxiety about her mother's well being. She cut the sandwich in half diagonally, put it on Jimmy's favorite blue plate, and took it to the dining cove.

"Here you go, Jack", she said absently."

Where was her older sister, Maddie? If she had someone she could talk to she would be able to discharge some of her angst. Annie, who was much weaker from her heart condition than she showed, might put on a tough exterior at times, but inside she was often terrified. Today was one of those days. Looking out the window toward the street, she noticed that sunlight had already started to fade. Annie was becoming more and more anxious. Where could Mother be? It was getting close to the time that Father usually came from work. He would be furious if supper wasn't ready. She had no more than put Jimmy's empty plate in the sink when she heard a car pull into the carport.

"Oh no!" she thought. "It will be really bad when Father realizes Mother isn't where she's supposed to be." Her stomach knotted, her insides trembled, and her mouth went dry with fear.

The door burst open, and Lorraine, shoved by Max, stumbled through the door. At least Annie assumed it was her mother. The woman with matted black hair, swollen eyes and face, and torn, wrinkled clothes looked familiar. Could that really be their mother? It *was* her mother! Annie's fear turned to anger.

Jack flew into a rage, flailing at his father, his hero, with his little fists, demanding to know what happened to his mother. Max put up with the little one's tirade for awhile, then without a word of warning drew his hand back and swung at the side of his son's head sending him nearly all the way across the living room. Too stunned to cry, Jimmy, wide-eyed, sat up holding his hand over his ear, unable to believe his father would hurt him so badly.

Max shoved Lorraine to their bedroom and slammed the door shut. Shouting and muffled sobs came from the room, along with Lorraine's pleas for forgiveness. Finally Max quieted down. The last words the children heard him shouting were "Don't you ever *dare* make me leave work again to rescue you!"

Later that night Annie emerged from the sanctuary of her bedroom to use the bathroom just as Max opened the door to her parents' room. He glared at her, mumbling something about "that black witch!" Annie lashed out at him in the most vile way she could think of. She spat at him. It didn't land on him, but his face swelled with rage. His green eyes widened, surrounded by red lids. Max turned around with fists clenched, and went back to the bedroom. Doctors had told him it could kill her if he ever hurt her, that they would see him prosecuted if he harmed her.

Annie couldn't sleep, worried about her mother and still shaking from the confrontation with her father. The sobs from her parent's had stopped for some time, and everything seemed calm and peaceful. She slipped out of bed and went quietly to her parent's room to see if her mother was ok. Peaking around the corner, she was shocked at what she saw. She fled to her room, confused, unable to understand what she had just seen. Climbing onto her bed, she wrapped her arms around her knees, shaking. She had heard whispered talk about 'what married people do in bed', but had never really known exactly what that was. She knew it was supposed to be a very special way to show love. What she saw totally confused her. How did what she had just seen make sense after seeing her mother beaten and bruised?

Her mother and father were wrapped around each other, making cooing sounds. She had seen her mother naked.

On top.

JOE IS DYING

1949

Annie came in to that dreaded emptiness that children experience when they come home and no one is there. She called out, but there was no answer. She didn't know where her mother or her brother had gone; there was just a vague lifeless pall. She went into the kitchen to get her favorite snack: three Nabisco soda crackers spread with Skippy peanut butter and half a glass of milk. Finishing her repast, she took her glass to rinse it out, and found a folded note on the yellow ceramic tile counter:

"We are in Artesia. Granddad had a stroke. Don't know when we will be back."

The words made Annie's mind race, her heart pound. How long would she be alone with her father? Max had never hurt her, but with her mother away, how would he vent his frustrations? She carefully did her assigned chores, especially making sure the front lawn was watered thoroughly. She used the 'T' handle to turn on the three 'x' shaped brass sprinkler valves that activated the underground watering system. When she saw that there was one spot that didn't get any water, she turned off the other two valves, leaving the one open that was closest to the arid area. She made certain that valve was wide open, but the one dry spot simply couldn't be reached. It worried her because it could be easily seen from the walk. She sighed, turned off the water, and went in the house. Maybe her father would use the side door, and wouldn't see the offending arid spot.

Max slumped over the steering wheel of the big black Buick, tightly gripping the plasticized pearl orb, his fingers white-clenched. He could barely breathe. He looked absently at his work-hardened hands: creases and fingernails irrevocably filled with grease from car engines he had worked on. Joe's hands were always clean, the fingernails always well groomed. His father-in-law never smelled like gasoline and motor oil. Slamming the wheel with one palm, he turned the key with the other then put the big black Buick into first gear. He motioned to one of his mechanics, and the man who did custom detailing on the Cadillacs, Continentals and Rolls Royces of the regular Miracle Mile customers.

"Gotta make a quick run", he waved and smiled as he sped out of the spotless red cement yard, bouncing onto New Hampshire Avenue. Just minutes before, his wife Lorraine had called to tell him her dad was dying.

"He's my dad, too," he thought bitterly. He pulled over and slammed on his brakes half way down the block. "What am I going to do now? Joe is my *friend*!"

Looking automatically in the rear view mirror, he waited for an oncoming car then pulled back onto the street. As if programmed to making the turns, the car seemed to automatically head for his long time mistress' apartment. Shaking with emotion, he banged on Marsha's door, certain he would find comfort on the other side. There was no answer. He pounded angrily on the wood casing until his hand hurt, finally letting it drop to his side in resignation. Aware of a neighbor scowling from a window, he shook his fist at the old man. "I pay for this place! I can do whatever the hell I please".

Back in the car, Max's head fell to his chest, stuffing his fists into his eyes to quell the tears trying to gush from his eyes. Spent from his fit of fury, his mind released a scramble of memories. Joe, his father-in-law, the only man he really looked up to was dying. Joe, the tall quiet Quaker, who never seemed to be ruffled or angry. Except for the time he made the mistake of flying into a rage in front of his in-laws, threatening Lorraine. Max had grabbed his young son under his arm, stormed out the kitchen door and slammed it so hard he broke out the window. He couldn't remember what he had been so mad about. But Joe threatened him. Joe the calm, the patient. Max couldn't bear thinking of the look in Joe's eyes. He wanted so desperately to have Joe's approval. And now this man of God would no longer be in his life. Max remembered how much he wanted to be like his father-in-law.

He flashed back to his childhood. All the moving from state to state with his mother and three siblings; following his philandering father. His older brother left home very young, leaving Max the only one to help their mother. His younger brother and sister had no inclination for work. He remembered carrying coal in the winter and hauling water from a well to make a little money for food from the time he was five. His mother was the only person outside of Marsha who ever appreciated his hard work. He started to feel sorry for himself, taking out a flask of whiskey he kept in the glove box.

"I have tried so hard all my life to be good enough! It has never mattered what I did. It was never enough. Fur coats weren't good enough. Expensive table settings and silverware weren't enough to make Lorraine happy. No wonder I take off with Marsha. He clenched his fists wanting one more time to feel Lorraine's flesh melt under his power. Make her care. Keep her from walking away. Make her grateful for all she had, thanks to his hard work.

He calmed down after his solitary tirade. "Annie will be home alone, so I might as well go see how she is doing", he decided. He had driven toward his home without much thought, not knowing whether he would actually go there. Home. It didn't matter what he did when he got there. He tried to be what he thought everyone there wanted – happy and fun. Nothing ever worked. He would park down the street and come to the living room window and make scary faces. Or he would pull the wolf whistle he had installed in the car to signal his arrival. He even took off his sweat soaked work sox and shoved them in Annie's face until she squealed and giggled. Shouldn't his kids run out and laugh and welcome him home? Fly into his arms, give him hugs and kisses? His fist slammed on the arm rest in his bitter disappointment.

Some nights he couldn't muster up the emotional energy it took to put on a show. Those nights came unexpectedly to the family, so they were always prepared for the worst. They never knew when he would come in raging. They were always tense. There was no way they could enjoy his antics for fear they would escalate in violence.

Max turned onto Andover Drive, where they lived in a neighborhood that had originally been scheduled to be the UCLA campus. The streets were wide with ample grassy parking strips and large flowering magnolia trees. It was a mostly new neighborhood. A couple of older homes had relinquished their isolation and new homes were built around them. There was the doctor on the corner and the movie star on the next street. Both had exquisite homes: one old Spanish style with tile roof and veranda, the other an old English style with carefully trimmed junipers.

As Max pulled into the driveway, he surveyed his well manicured home. At least Lorraine was a good gardener and housekeeper. He had to admit she, too, was a hard worker. If only she wasn't so bitter. She should be happy, since because of him she had such a nice place to live. Stepping between the tree roses that lined the winding walk that led to the front porch, he checked to see if Annie had watered the lawn. He spied a place that was dry. The spot that Annie could not get the sprinklers to reach. Suddenly his anger returned.

"Joe's dying, I'm hurting, and Annie can't even do the one thing she was supposed to do! She stands up to me when everyone else just cowers. She even spit at me one time after . . . oh, yeah, I did mess up her mother pretty bad that time. That doesn't give her a right to act that way. She'd better be a little more humble this time. I'm in no mood to put up with insolence."

A sudden thought of Joe caused him to hesitate by the door, his chest convulsing in the pain of loss. Annie was waiting, hands sweating, mouth dry - anxious to know which father would come into the house, the violent one or the loving one. She anxiously tried to read his face, but the mixture of emotion she saw confused her.

"I'm not a very good cook, but I tried to fix you something to eat," she said hesitantly. "You're home earlier than I expected."

"You didn't water the lawn!" Max raged.

"Yes, I did" Annie said, trying not to sound indignant.

"Right there at the end of the porch where you can see the ground is dry. You did not water the lawn."

"Yes, I did. The sprinklers don't reach that one spot" she answered evenly, noting the red rising from Max's neck to his cheeks.

Without warning, he grabbed her by the arm and dragged her into the kitchen, pulling out a chair with his free hand. He threw her over his knee as he sat down and hit her bottom violently until he released enough anger to calm down. He let her go, sitting there looking lost.

"Your Granddad is dying. Joe is dying." He didn't look at Annie, he just got up and went to bed.

Annie had never been physically hurt by anyone before, and it made her really angry to think her father would take out his upset on her. She refused to cry while he was beating her, and she refused to cry after he was finished.

INCINERATED

1956

Every morning, Annie walked the ten blocks to the bus stop where she boarded the bus for South Central Los Angeles. The two and a half hour trip on bus and streetcar took her through the Cahuenga Pass to Hollywood, where she boarded another bus that went close to downtown Los Angeles. Then a twenty minute wait for the streetcar on Vermont Avenue, an often frightening area which only a few years later was on the fringe of the Watts riots. On more than one occasion big black shiny cars pulled up to the curb and gold-toothed men flashing big diamond rings offered obscene suggestions for her day's activities. While this was a bit unnerving, and she did get frightened at times, she never showed fear. She simply took up the habit of walking to the next stop, or the next, until she heard the clacking of the streetcar wheels approaching. She was going to college. That was more important than worrying about silly men in big cars.

The tiny college campus had art-deco styled buildings with rounded corners that looked like stylized waterfalls. A goldfish-filled round pond with a fountain in the center was the focal point: all the broad walkways converged there, making it a frequent meeting place. The auditorium and classroom buildings were on the south, and the dorms on the north. The palm tree lined Promenade passed the boys' and girls' dorms separated by the cafeteria. On the far end, and across the street, the gymnasium stood next to the small building which held the clinic and health related classrooms.

Her favorite classroom was on the east side of the auditorium: the art class. Reached by graceful stairs with artistic metal railings, the classroom looked out over the campus. With but one instructor, there was little opportunity for students to get even a minor in art. But Mrs. Welch took the class on numerous field trips to give them exposure to many art forms. Once they went to the Los Angeles County Museum to an exhibit of Modern Art. With little experience viewing abstract paintings, many of the students giggled at what appeared to be a nonsensical mixture of angles and splashes of clashing colors. A couple of 'artsy' students stood back, hands stroking chins in an attitude of appreciation. Annie was in the first group.

Between trips were sessions of drawing specific subjects. Annie especially liked the exercises that incorporated perspective. The converging of lines which gave depth to a subject was very satisfying. There were two young men about her age who had mastered drawing realistic, if futuristic, automobiles. She envied their ability to make the cars look like they could be driven off the page.

There were other field trips to art schools around the area. Mrs. Welch recognized that there were students in her classes whose talents exceeded her ability to guide. Trips to schools like Art Institute, located in an elegant, tree lined neighborhood was her favorite. It's quiet, sophisticated atmosphere appealed to some, but not to Annie. Not until the trip to Pasadena, and the Art Center College of Design did Annie find the place she wanted desperately to go.

They went from classroom to busy classroom. Rooms with clay dust on the floors, classrooms with the pungent odors of oil paints and turpentine, everywhere activity. Art being incorporated into usable objects. Art to make everyday life more beautiful. At each area visited, Annie thought "I would really like to do that."

At one classroom, her heart started to pound and her breath came in short, shallow gasps. Young men with carving tools shaped huge mounds of clay into life-sized models of cars. Each stroke curled off smooth slices of moist clay. "These are the future designers for General Motors, Ford and Chrysler," she thought. Off to one side was another, smaller group, crafting versions of European sports cars. She could hardly contain her enthusiasm, blurting out that this is where she wanted to be. Snickers came from the boys in the group. "Do you see any *girls* in there", sneered one. She gave him a dirty look, and determined that somehow she would manage to join that elite group. Her passion for cars began early in life, spending time at her dad's upscale service station on Wilshire Boulevard. Now she knew how to channel that love.

On the way out, Mrs. Welch encouraged them to stop at the registrar's office to get information on requirements, tuition, and possible scholarships. While the others kept up a constant chatter on the way back to he college. Annie was in deep thought. How could she manage to afford Art Center? Would the art work she had done over the years satisfy the portfolio requirement? Of the former, she had grave doubts as to the ability to garner funds to enroll. But she felt that the artwork she had saved, minus the drawing the Red Cross had taken to be shown around the world, should suffice.

All the way back to the college, and the two and a half hours travel time home, all she could think of was getting covered with clay shavings, and lines made smooth and graceful by her own hands. She could barely keep from running the ten blocks back home. She couldn't wait to tell her mother of the trip, and her desire to design cars.

Annie rushed into the house to find her mother, but she wasn't there. Lorraine often spent time out on the patio after work, and that's where Annie headed. "Mother!" she called, unable to squelch her enthusiasm. Her mother wasn't on the patio, but out in the yard, putting paper into the incinerator. Smoke poured from the little chimney. "Mother", she called again. "Guess what! We went to Art Center today! I have to go there! They design cars and all sorts of wonderful things!"

Lorraine looked up from her task, pushing the last paper into the fire. As it went, Annie could see it was one of her paintings.

"What are you doing?" she cried.

"Cleaning out the garage", Lorraine replied. Annie saw the empty portfolio folder on the ground. As empty as the expression on her mother's face.

"But I need my artwork!" she cried. "I can't get into Art Center without it!" "

"Art Center? What's that about? Oh, well, you can always do more."

Annie ran to the garage. Everything was neatly arranged as it always was. She hesitantly approached the shelf which had held her portfolio, nearly empty now. But not quite. There were the few pieces of art that her brother and sister had brought home from school, but hers were all missing. She felt weak. It seemed as if her arms had been cut off. She went back outside.

"Why did you do that? You didn't burn anything but *my* work! *Why*?" she sobbed.

Lorraine just shrugged her shoulders and walked back to the house.

Annie felt dead, her dreams destroyed.

Incinerated.

A Conversation with Myself

April still surprises me.
The veil falls, and I wonder where it comes from
Colors fade along with my sense of self
Everything I do seems worthless
Even with others around I am alone

This year differs from the years before,
the little girl materializes in my heart.
She demands attention.

"It is me, the child left in a metal-barred crib."

But that was many years ago, I tell her.

"I have come to the door of your mind,
bringing down a curtain of gloom, hoping
you would finally listen to yourself.
Every year I come.
I stay the same age I was in that crib.
it was not the isolated incident of being left alone for so long.
It started long before."

I often feel alone, not knowing why.

"You need to remember a few things:
you hid in the back yard, hoping Daddy would ask for you.
He took our brother with him, but Mother always said
he didn't want you.

And what about all those days you cut school
spending the days in mindless sweeping
as if cleaning the floor would banish your pain.
How about Mother's co-worker who wanted
to take pictures of you?
You quickly realized that he was looking for a porn model
and you refused.
Mother said you were lying, what would she say to him?
He might be mad at her.
She was ashamed that you told him to take pictures
of his own wife in that sheer negligee."

"You came home from babysitting when you were 16 years old
to find the house cold and empty
You looked all over the house and yard, but no one was there;
the car still in the garage.
There was no note of explanation.
You waited and waited but no one came.
Did something terrible happen to them, you fretted.
Surely our brother had just gone to a friend's
He would come home and you wouldn't be alone.
Mother never came, your brother never came.
You finally went to sleep, certain you would
Wake to find them home.

You woke alone that day and the next day and the next.
What had happened to our little family?
On the fourth day, the door flew open
there was Mother, bringing with her fresh outdoor air
and a huge smile.
"We had so much fun at Tahoe, didn't we son?"
"Tahoe?" you asked.
"Yes, Fogel took us."
" No one told me".

"I guess I forgot."
She took off her coat
and collapsed on the couch with a satisfied sigh.

"But you thought the gloom was your own fault."
I have tried every year to make you understand.
"It wasn't you, it wasn't your fault."

Tears, the tears I had held in all those years
poured from my eyes, withheld sobs shook my body.

"Finally you hear me" my young self said.

I take her face in my hands looking into her eyes,
I love you, I tell her.

"That's only the beginning of the stories, you know."

I answer with a nod.
I hold her close and tell her how precious she is.
I cry until this day's pain is drained away.

"When I come back next year there will be more
stories for you to remember,"

I know. I will answer you when you knock.

PART II

On The Bus

1948

Walking swiftly through the park, Annie was anxious to get to the intersection. She hurried through the park to get to the bus stop where San Fernando Road and Scott Road crossed. Although it was a spectacular summer morning with sparrow and blackbird chicks sweetly demanding food, and a soft breeze causing the leaves of the overhanging trees to flutter, reflecting brilliant sunlight; she didn't notice. Her attention was focused solely on getting to the bus stop on the far side of the intersection. Bernadine, a friend she hadn't seen for several years was going to meet her in Glendale. She was anxious to see her since they became teenagers.

Coming out onto the sidewalk, she was surprised by the brilliance of the sun and the intense heat rising from the sidewalk and asphalt roadway. Impatiently looking from side to side for a break in traffic, she feared the bus would come before she could get across to the patch of shade in front of the little dime store where the 'Bus Stop' sign was planted. She finally got safely across and drew a deep breath, thankful the bus hadn't arrived leaving her stranded. Then she realized she had forgotten to bring a book to read in transit. She always remembered to bring a book so that she wouldn't appear to be open for conversation. She didn't have enough money to buy a hardback, and in the early '50's the only paperbacks she knew of were on the order of 'Lady

Chatterly's Lover'. Not the sort of book the shy young girl wanted to be seen reading.

She went into the store on the chance she might find something she wouldn't be ashamed to be seen reading. Turning the book tower slowly to peruse the titles, she scanned two rows before seeing a title that seemed safe: *The Imitation of Christ.* Opening it to a the Table of Contents, the chapter titles were very much to her liking, reflecting spiritual ideas that were germinating in her questing young mind. Quickly paying for the tome, she hurried out in time to see the big grey bus with 'Glendale' in bold letters approaching from the north.

After paying the fare, she looked around to find a seat away from everyone, near the back. She sat next to the aisle to avoid anyone sitting next to her. Settling in, she randomly opened her new book. Unprepared for what she read, she dropped the book to her lap, thoughts tumbling over one another. What if what she read was true? Raised in a fundamentalist church, she followed their strict Biblical interpretations, believing them to be absolutely true. But after today, those few sentences would forever change one of the most defining parts of her religious upbringing.

Such an innocent appearing title: "The Imitation of Christ". How much she wanted to do just that: imitate Christ. At the tender age of fifteen, she had the idealism of many young people, and the confidence in God that made such a thing seem possible. *To truly receive the body and blood of Jesus.* The title of one of the chapters.

Could that be?

Yet there it was, in black and white, printed on paper, written centuries ago and believed by millions. But most of all, it resonated in her mind and heart. She determined, by the time the bus driver called out her stop, to test out her new belief, temporarily forgetting about Bernadine. She stepped down to the sidewalk and saw Bernadine. She gave Annie an enthusiastic hug. Annie absentmindedly hugged her back. She had just spent a half hour contemplating a deep spiritual concept.

Annie made a plan: once in awhile, her mother didn't go to church. Annie would pick one of. these days, look for a pew where no one would sit either beside her or in back of her, then see if Jesus would make his Presence known. The Sunday finally came. Her mother wasn't well and her little brother had gone to the beach with their father. Annie showered and put on her best blue dress, combed out the curls from the rollers she had slept with. She was going to meet Jesus. She knew that He would be there.

After walking in the damp light rain to the church, she deliberately went in a bit late, standing at the back to check how people were dispersed. There was Mrs. Spelling with her big wide brimmed yellow hat in the second row. Her husband was one of the deacons, and she always wore the finest clothes. And, she was the only lady who wore obvious makeup. It was difficult for other lady parishioners to keep from gossiping. A few more rows of regulars: families with little children, and some little old ladies smelling of talc.

Then she saw what she was looking for - three rows with no one sitting near the aisle. It was on the opposite side from where their little family usually sat. With heart pounding from the walk and anticipation, she slipped into the middle pew. She made a place for Jesus. And she waited for Him to come. The sermon seemed interminable – she was waiting for the Communion Service. Then the collection plate was sent around. She didn't know how Jesus would show Himself to her, but she would be terribly disappointed if he didn't.

Finally, the Communion plates, one with unleavened bread and the other with tiny glass cups with grape juice came to Annie. She carefully broke off a piece of the flat, lightly baked bread. Then she drank the grape juice. And she closed her eyes, something no one but one old man who sat down front ever did. And she bowed her head and waited. It was a grey day, but when she closed her eyes, it was like bright sunshine. She peeked to see if the sun was out, but it was still steely looking. She closed her eyes again. And it was bright as before.

Annie repeated it once more, with the same amazing results.

Then someone touched her shoulder. "Jesus!" she thought. She could scarcely breathe. Shivers of excitement ran through her. "It's true!" She opened her eyes and looked around her. No one was close. But she knew she felt the touch. She knew she would remember that touch until the day she died.

After that day, she always believed that Jesus was present in the bread and the grape juice. When the minister said the words "This is not the body of Christ, but for a remembrance only" and "This is not the blood of Christ, but for a remembrance only", Annie only smiled to herself:

"Yes, it is."

Cora

1983

Annie looked up just as the shelter door opened. A tiny, raw-boned lady, obviously agitated, rushed into the office.

"They took my daughter from school, and didn't tell me anything about it," she sputtered.

Annie had never seen the woman before, and it was clear she was beyond upset, she was indignantly furious. This was Annie's introduction to Cora. It seems her daughter reported that her father, Jack, had been molesting her for a long time. The school had called Social Services, and Debbie was immediately taken and put in a foster care home. But this was only the beginning of the story.

Cora had grown up in an abusive family; her dad had molested her for years before she ran away. Because of her history, she said she never left her daughter alone with Jack. There wasn't any time when he could have touched Debbie. Obviously, that wasn't Debbie's experience.

Cora's life was one Annie was involved with over a period of several years. She hadn't an ounce of fat on her body, and she had the muscular look of one who had known more than her share of work. Her large teeth were obviously in need of a dentist, but she was always clean, neat and attractive. She smelled of clothes fresh off the line: spotless knife crease jeans and feminine blouses. Something about her blustery personality made Annie like her immediately. She so sincerely cared for her children, fiercely insisting on supporting and caring for them.

"They said Jack has to leave before Debbie can come home! I have to make him leave! But I love him, and I know he couldn't do those things! I never leave them alone!"

She told what a broken man he had become when he backed over his oldest son, killing him. How she had comforted him through that sorrow. Well, yes, he was abusive once in awhile, hitting her and being too hard on the kids. But she was tough, she said, she fought back. And no, Jack didn't work much of the time. But she was strong. She could work, her job at the laundry paid pretty well, fleshing out what she got from the county. But it would be hard if Jack left. He helped her with the boys.

Annie tried to give her food, but she wouldn't take that, or any money. She would have to report it to Social Services. She was scrupulously honest. Annie took her to the police station, where she filled out the complaint to have Jack removed. It was hard for her, but that was the process she had to go through so Debbie could come home.

When they went to court for Jack's molestation trial, Annie noticed he had his name imprinted on the back of his belt. It was something that became almost the Badge of Perpetrators: in court the vast majority them had their name prominently displayed on their shirt or belt.

Jack got three years in prison.

It is hard to describe Cora. She talked, laughed a lot, and was generally passionate about life. And she made the most amazing malapropisms. They always seemed to explain a situation better than the *correct* word. Annie kept a notepad in a drawer just to capture some of her amazing verbiage. Annie's favorite was when she called to tell her that her son Brian had been diagnosed with '*screwliosis*' - scoliosis, a twisting of the spine, which sounded like a better way to describe the disease.

Her troubles didn't end with Debbie's return to the fold. Her son, Sammy, was labeled slow, he had difficulty in school. He was given a free pass to the YMCA pool, and there he met up with a city alderman and his proctologist friend. These two pillars of the community enjoyed swimming under the water, grabbing boys' genitals. They liked watching the boys dress, and the ones who were chosen as 'special' were filmed naked, and got to drink beer and watch porno movies at the alderman's house. All the chosen boys were mentally slow.

Sammy and his friend came to the shelter office and told Annie about all they had been exposed to. The boys were very upset, feeling like somehow it was their fault. The boys, Cora and Annie went to the police station, where they reported the two men. Cora was her usual blustery self, incensed at the men's vile behavior.

Because the boys couldn't remember dates, or specifically where the incidents happened, the doctor got off. The alderman was simply restricted from any contact with anyone under 18 for three years. But they did have the satisfaction of slapping his fingers.

Over the years, Cora continued to keep Annie informed about her life, and what was going on with her children. She admitted to sneaking off to be with Jack on occasion, but she did keep him away from the children. She saw to it that they all got good mental health care, and the unfailing love of a passionate mother.

THE SIX WOMEN WERE PACKED IN LIKE SOFT TOMATOES.

NEXT: THE PROPHET

AFTER THE SPIRIT – PROPHET

1963

The small blue sedan followed the undulations of the two lane highway leading to the high desert. Up and down through the gusts of sand that rushed across their path to a date with the sacred. Heat, rising from the pavement, created shimmering mirages.

Eleanor, their transporter, heard of a man living in the desert who, it was claimed, had the gift of prophecy. He was very poor, and he and his wife lived by faith. They were totally dependent on the generosity of others. In return they ministered to all who called upon them, sharing their faith and laying hands on the sick.

The six women were packed in like soft tomatoes. They were on their way to meet the Prophet. An air of excitement filled the car, and all but one was formulating questions that would prompt him to give them a word of wisdom. Discussion centered on receiving a prophecy about their future, or an answer to a current problem. Annie, who sat next to the window behind Eleanor, the driver, was the lone skeptic. At least she could look out at the changing scenery and think her own thoughts.

The air conditioner gave little relief to those in back. The windows were rolled up to keep the cool conditioned air in, and the blowing dust out. All of the women were dressed in variations of '60's polyester: hot and irritating to the skin. But no one noticed the discomfort in their pilgrimage expectations.

All of the women had one thing in common: they had recently experienced a phenomenon called baptism in the Holy Spirit. They met weekly to pray and share the spiritual insights they gained during the previous week. There would be singing, sharing of Scripture, and praying in tongues as experienced in the early Church.

As they drove, Annie reflected on the genesis of this trip with these Spirit-seeking women. She was the one, who as usual, sought out new ideas, new experiences, and was the first of the group who had been prayed over. She had sought out the lone Catholic Charismatic prayer group in Southern California after reading an article about the fresh movement of the Holy Spirit at Duquesne University. Annie went alone to her first meeting at a home near the Southern California coast.

Paradoxically, the intellectually bold young mother of five became shy when it came to facing the reality of her boldness. It was the first of many meetings she would attend, bringing with her Mary, who was as intellectually skeptical as Annie was about what was going on, whether it was a true experience or one that was deceptively false. So true, so heartfelt and spiritually fulfilling were their experiences, that more and more of their friends became involved.

The movement grew quickly, and soon priests came under the influence of the Holy Spirit while attending the prayer meetings. Each person who chose to do so was prayed over for the purpose of receiving the Holy Spirit and healing. Those meetings lasted far into the night, with joyful melodies and praying and singing in 'tongues'. It was reminiscent of what is recorded in the book of Acts, when the early Christians met together.

As they rode, city turned to suburbs, then to country. Small ranches with big gardens and corrals with horses changed to barren land where only cactus and sagebrush grew. A few tired houses were scattered in the distance, broken windmills at their side.

After several more miles, the road was scoured by waves of

sandy soil that restlessly blew, unhindered by vegetation. Through a break in the blowing sand, a small house with what appeared to be an old one-room school house came into view. Slowing down, Eleanor turned into what seemed to be a driveway, gingerly guiding the car down the rutted one lane road.

It opened up into a large area that could accommodate a number of vehicles. That day, theirs was the only car to be seen. The house was to the left. It had probably been white at some time, but most of the paint had peeled off. What was left had taken on the color of the sandy soil. A single large tree shaded the house.

Straight ahead was an old barn, its sagging doors swinging back and forth with the wind. Remnants of red paint hung in shreds from the warped boards. Two scrawny dun colored dogs lay in the sun, while several chickens scratched hopefully for worms. There was no visible form of transportation, and no apparent farm implements.

On the right was, indeed, an old one room school house. Eight steps went up to the classroom. It was in better condition than the other two structures, bearing a coat of white paint. It was no doubt where they would meet with Prophet.

Everyone got out of the car, gratefully stretching cramped muscles and straightening wrinkled clothing. Eleanor, the owner and driver of the car and in her early forties, was a bit matronly. She had a short practical haircut that fit her busy lifestyle which included her husband, 4 children and 3 foster children.

Mary was tall and slim with short graying hair that curled around her face. She had three children, and was the intellectual of the group. Her husband was a scientist who was working on a top-secret communications project.

The women often met at her house, sometimes with larger groups in the evening.

The most emotional of the six was Maria. She and her husband Jose were deeply involved in the new spirituality, and had been known to have ecstatic outpourings of their faith. They had left the Catholic Church and worshipped with their son and his friends in a small Pentecostal church.

Ernestine was from Nicaragua, married to, and then divorced from, an Anglo. She was excitable and her colorful clothes reflected her vibrant personality. She retained her beautiful accent and sometimes indecipherable exclamations. It was at her home that their little group had been the first to hear the hymn 'Come to the Water'. It was written by three young people the night before. They had all had a spiritual experience which had caused them to give up drugs. When they sang the last words, 'that for those tears I died', all present had tears.

Charlotte was new to the group, and they knew very little about her. She was divorced, and she was ostracized by many in the church. She was blonde and slim with perfect features and a beautiful body. Busy women with small children and virile husbands felt threatened by her presence.

For several minutes, the women stood in the midday heat, not sure whether or not to knock on the door. To pass the time, Eleanor opened the car's trunk and started arranging the food they had all gathered in compatible stacks for easy hauling. There were boxes full of Kraft Macaroni and Cheese, cans of Span, Libby's Corned Beef, Pop Tarts, Wheaties, and a variety of canned fruits and vegetables

Soon they heard a screen door open. Out stepped a woman wearing a long dress and a full apron. She had her grey hair pulled back in a bun. Her slow movements and the deep sun dried creases in her face gave the impression of a very old woman.

"Greetings' she said in a strong, sweet voice which belied her age. 'God bless you for coming. We always treasure a visit from God's children. Prophet will be out shortly.' She had barely uttered her greeting when a thin wiry old man emerged from the same door. He had a bit of white beard, which looked more like a need to shave than an intentional decoration. He wore black work pants held up by rainbow colored suspenders. His faded blue shirt sleeves were rolled up, no doubt because of the intense desert heat.

The feature which drew one to him most was his eyes. Dark and penetrating, they were shaded by heavy brows. He looked like the descriptions of Old Testament prophets. His very appearance created tension. No wonder he was called 'Prophet'. Annie would feel the intense heat of those eyes before the day was over.

"We have a few things for you" Eleanor said breaking the momentary spell. 'Can we help you take them in? " Both Prophet and his wife nodded yes. So Mary, Maria and Eleanor carried the boxes of food into the house, led by Mrs. Prophet. They never knew their names.

When the women came back out, Prophet, having put on a dusty black jacket, asked all the women to join him in the schoolhouse-church. There were ten pews on either side of the simple chapel, and a small pulpit in front. The walls were white, bare; and there was no ornamentation of any kind. Everything was flawlessly clean except where a film of sand had blown in under the door.

Prophet sat on a straight chair next to the podium, head down and eyes closed. He remained still for what became an uncomfortably long time before looking up to heaven and prayed for the Holy Spirit to fall upon the little assembly.

Prophet spoke to them of Jesus and his command to love and care for one another, praising the women for their generosity. He reminded them that Jesus had told the disciples that He had to die so that the Holy Spirit could come to them. The Spirit would comfort them and teach them those things they needed to know to live fulfilled and holy lives. Having started out gently, he changed his style abruptly, warning of false teachings and lack of perseverance in the true path laid out by Jesus. He finished with a prayer of thanksgiving and sat back down.

When he stood back up, he began that part of the meeting that most of the women had come for. He asked if anyone had any questions. He explained that while God had given him certain gifts, they would be manifest only as the Holy Spirit prompted. The women looked at each other; tacitly acknowledging Eleanor's right to be first. Annie sat alone near the back, since she didn't plan on asking a question.

Eleanor wanted to know if God would be using her for any special work. Prophet said that we all have special work to do, and anything done in Jesus' name would be special. He told her that everything done in His name was filled with God's love, and therefore truly good. Three more of the women asked similar questions, receiving the same sort of answer. They all nodded to each other in agreement with his statements, each one basking in having received a special word from Prophet.

The fifth woman, Maria, started to ask her question when suddenly Prophet's whole appearance changed. He straightened up, and as if struck by some invisible force, stretched out his hand and pointed to the back of the chapel toward Annie, as if he had just realized she was back there. The women turned to see what he was pointing at.

Annie turned to see if there was something behind her. When she saw that nothing unusual was to be seen, she turned back around and looked into the blazing eyes of Prophet. His finger was pointed directly at her.

"You!" he shouted. "You are going to be like a tree planted beside the water.

"Many people will come under the spreading branches of that tree, and will be filled with your fruit!" His brows lowered and his voice became intense "But first, you must lose your pride!"

There was complete silence. The old man dropped his hand, his whole body sagging. He went back to the simple altar and said that he was finished for the day, thanking everyone for coming. Maria's question went unanswered.

In near silence, the women went down the stairs and got in the car. The busy conversations on the trip to Prophet's were muted on the way home. The wind was still blowing the sand across the asphalt, and heat mirages still hung on the road. One woman would never forget this day.

Annie sat by the window watching the changing scenes. She pondered Prophet's words, wondering if there was any truth in what he said. It was only when she became an old woman, remembering, that she knew.

The Lesson

1962

Maybe all the years of being solitary because of her frail health, or maybe because of her Nana's spiritual influence, Annie occasionally experienced God in unique, sometimes surprising ways. How do you explain being touched by God: it can't really been done.

She always questioned, sometimes verging on heresy. One of her questions regarded the crucifixion. Having experienced a great deal of pain as a result of two heart surgeries and the agonizing cough associated with frequent bronchial pneumonia growing up, she had difficulty understanding the focus on the pain Jesus experienced on the cross. She felt guilty about her cavalier attitude about His suffering, but had total reverence for her savior's willingness to do whatever necessary to obtain the salvation of all mankind. It had not yet become personal to her, as much as she longed for and prayed for such a realization. She was never surprised when she experienced the holy Presence. Not by the time, the place, or the manifestation.

It was still dark in the kitchen when Annie clicked on the light under the copper colored hood over the gas stovetop. She removed a container of chicken livers from the refrigerator, flouring them in readiness for frying. They were a part of her husband Craig's favorite breakfast. Over the sound of the shower, she heard a little creak of the crib where their youngest son slept. A faint thump on the linoleum signaled little Steve had landed, ready for a running start on the day. As expected, he came flying into the kitchen, simultaneously slamming into his mother's leg and throwing his arms around her thighs. He smiled up at her, eyes twinkling, pointing at the stove. "Me, me" he said. He loved fried chicken livers and cherished eating them with his dad.

Up to this time, all was as usual. She had put the ingredients for tiger's milk in the blender: frozen orange juice, powdered milk, brewers yeast, wheat germ, and enough skim milk to whirl the nutritious brew. It was loved by both of the early rising males.

Annie lifted the expectant little one into his high chair and turned back to the task at hand, frying chicken livers to perfection. She caught a faint hint of a second odor over the pungent aroma of the frying meat. At first she couldn't identify it. Oddly, it smelled like fresh wood. She looked around for a source of the odor, but it was summer; no fire wood was in the house. She could only assume this was not an earthly odor. Was God speaking to her in a new way? At first she assumed it was her imagination. But it not only didn't go away, it became stronger. So, she simply thanked God for this awareness, and humbly asked for its purpose.

As she cooked, a sensation of a square rough log seemed to pierce clear through her chest. She didn't question the sensation, visualizing it her mind, seemingly very real. It didn't hinder her movements, but she was continually aware of its presence. She believed, as she had first suspected, that this was another kind of teaching from God: real to her, but unseen by others. She believed in time she would come to understand when she finally understood its meaning. Soon another faint odor mingled with the wood, the sweet smell of fresh blood. Confusion could be an understatement of these unusual sensations. And yet they were very real to her: seeing in her mind's eye the shape and roughness of the wood, feeling the heavy roughness of its bulk, and the palpably pungent odor of the blood. As she went about her daily work, she prayed that God would reveal to her what she was to learn, what meaning it had. All through that day, the next, and the next, the fragrant log in her, painless but with a persistent reminder of its presence. Everywhere she went, it was there: when she made the beds, when she washed clothes, when she bathed the children, cooked the dinner, it was there. Late on the third day it inexplicably went away.

Annie was so busy taking care of five little children that she didn't assess her experience. When she finally took the time to look back on the three days, she became aware of a truth she had sought: Jesus' death on the cross was more than the suffering, even though that was certainly true. She finally, belatedly, realized what Jesus' crucifixion was all about, one that she would remember all her life:

The lesson was love. Love, even for her!

LOVE AND TRUST

1983

Annie was staring out the window, absentmindedly washing dishes from the night before. By the time dinner was over, Annie was so tired she often left dishes for the next morning. There was something soothing about having her hands in warm water She saw her children off on the school bus after the usual early morning complaints: 'she took my skirt'; 'I don't like to eat breakfast!' If only those minor irritations were all she had to deal with. Her older teen age children were unmanageable, partying and getting into trouble at school and with the authorities. They were disrespectful, often using the foul language that was so offensive to her.

She and her husband Craig lived outside the city with their five children. So the quiet that ensued when everyone had left for the day was of the depth only the country can provide. She occasionally had what she called "visuals", wide awake experiences that others might consider figments of her imagination. But what she saw, what she felt, always held deep meaning for her.

It had rained in the night, and droplets still hung on the leaves of the cottonwoods outside the window. The grass, which withered in the late autumn heat, took on a fresh stance, standing straight and tall. It made Annie smile to see the wonderful changes brought about by the little storm. Maybe that's the way all life is, regenerated by little storms. She was drifting into a reflective mood, as she often did around water. Sometimes she was given insights which made an impact on her thinking, on her life.

Looking out the window, in her mind's eye, she saw herself walking down one of the main residential streets of town. On her back was a wicker basket with straps like a back pack. It was beautifully woven and finished in a rich brown. It fit her shoulders as if it was designed especially for her. As she examined it, she could see that its dimensions were the width of two sheets of typing paper side by side, a divider in the center. She saw that the basket was full of file folders, each with its own heading. Looking closer she saw that each heading corresponded with one of the many concerns she kept going over in her mind.

She seemed to be trying to get somewhere, but at every street corner she was unable to cross until she stopped, took off the basket, read and touched each heading; checking to make sure nothing was missing. Once the ritual was finished, she put the pack back on her shoulders and continued on her way to the next cross street. The whole process was repeated each time she came to a corner. It seemed obvious that the constant rehashing of her problems needed to stop. It wasn't making them go away or easier to bear. But she was comfortable with her little litany of problems and complaints.

The scene faded away, and Annie felt that she had at least gained insight into the depth of her need to change this habit. Just as she was beginning to think how to replace the habitual mental complaints, she sensed someone standing behind her. Close enough to feel warmth from a body. Whoever it might be, emanated love and compassion. She felt very peaceful.

Strong, gentle hands were placed on her shoulders. A man's voice softly said "My yoke is easy, and my burden is light." Smoothing his hands across her shoulders, he went on: "Hanging from *My* yoke are two buckets, one on either side. In one is love and in the other is trust. In the one you saw, all your worries and complaints. Every morning you have the option of picking up one burden: your basket of sorrow, defeat and anger, or my yoke with buckets full of love and trust. You must make that choice every morning. It is up to you to decide how you are going to live that day."

Annie breathed a sigh of submission. She vowed to never forget that gentle lesson. She often remembered the day when she learned that she had the power to decide how she would face each day. Most days she chose love and trust.

THE MEDICINE POUCH

1998

Nayette swaggered into the Patients' Library, wearing a flimsy see-through purple blouse and a short, tight fitting black skirt. Her eyes swept the room - a predator stalking her prey. She was searching for men. Annie watched her go from man to man, flirting and snuggling. A cloud of cheap perfume followed her as she strutted through the room. Annie was very protective of the men who came into the library: "my boys". Most were chemical dependency patients, and anyone who became too familiar with a member of the opposite sex was thrown out of treatment.

She immediately disliked her. She feared that one or more of the men would be sent home before finishing their treatment. Almost all of their patrons were Native Americans from various reservations: Spirit Lake, Standing Rock and Red Lake. There were also Gros Ventre, Assinaboine, and Chippewa. Before Nayette left the library, she got a Crow man to give her his medicine pouch. It had been given to him by his uncle, Standing Grey Wolf, from over in Montana.

One of Annie's duties was to train patient workers in library procedures. As she was leaving, she thought "I won't have her as a trainee!" She had never refused a patient, but Annie was prepared to this time. It was only a few days later that the director of the building came in to tell her that he had a new patient for to work with. And of course, it was Nayette. Annie said she wouldn't work with her; let her co-worker do it. He reminded Annie that this was part of her job description, and she *would* work with her.

Annie forced herself to remember that Nayette was a patient in a mental institution. It was not only her job, but her privilege to treat these people with respect, to help in their recovery. This was the first person that Annie had responded to this way.

She showed Nayette those things she would be doing: shelving books and 'reading' the shelves for books out of order. Annie asked her a little about herself. She said she was admitted for uncontrolled diabetes. Her legal guardian had gotten a court order which required her to be in a medical facility at all times. That way she would take her diabetic meds, and she would eat proper food. It was clear that she knew how to get her own way, even if it was harmful to her. Nayette was only 30 years old. Annie never really found out why she had a legal guardian.

Little by little, she disclosed some facts about herself. A Chippewa/Ojibwa from Minnesota, Nayette had few of the physical characteristics of Ojibwa women: slim, graceful bodies and thick, shiny dark hair of the Ojibwa and soft full lips of the French trapper ancestors. Nayette's hair was medium brown with little luster. She was about five feet tall, and she was a little heavy. Her father was German, and she had inherited many of his harsh physical characteristics. She displayed none of the modesty of Native women. A sad look came into her hazel eyes when she showed Annie pictures of her with her tall, dark sisters.

After about six weeks working in the library, Nayette was discharged. Annie got a better understanding of her behavior during that short time. She told Annie her father had given her first negligee to her when she was nine years old. By the time she was 18, he had taken her to Denver to perform as an exotic dancer. She talked about her penthouse apartment, how she walked along the edge of the wall surrounding the rooftop patio, high on drugs given to her by her promoter father. She didn't talk about what had happened in the intervening years except to mention her children: a boy and a girl living in Colorado. She was proud of the amount of money she made and the attention she had received from men. It was clear that being victimized by her father over the years was the basis for her overtly sexual behavior. She couldn't seem to focus on anything except the men who came to the library. Annie wasn't able to help her learn any skill. And so, she was a bit relieved when she learned Nayette was leaving.

Upon her release, Nayette was placed in an assisted living facility 40 miles north of where Annie lived. Annie got a call from the home saying Nayette could only leave with a staff member, her aging guardian – or Annie. Why she would put her on the list surprised Annie. She barely knew her. Didn't she have any trustworthy friend to take her out for an afternoon? A month after her move, Annie got a call. Nayette desperately wanted Annie to take her to Mass. Annie assumed that 'going to Mass' was one way of getting to leave the home. She knew it had to be hard for a young woman, living in a confined space with people fifty years her senior. Even though it meant missing Mass with her own family, Annie grudgingly said she would come take Nayette the following Sunday.

"Oh, by the way, would you bring some sage and sweet grass?" she asked. Annie replied that she would.

When she met her in the lobby, she seemed genuinely happy to see Annie.

"Did you bring the sage; did you bring the sweet grass? They won't let me have any here."

Annie replied that she had brought both. Nayette beamed. The way she was dressed concerned Annie. This was a very conservative community, and even though she was fresh and clean, her outfit was not the least bit conservative: white shorts and a sleeveless pink blouse that barely met her shorts. Annie's suggestion to change met deaf ears and a shrug. She didn't want Nayette to be stared at. Annie had begun to care.

It was clear by her behavior at the church that if she had

been baptized Catholic, she had not been taken to Mass very often. She wiggled and squirmed, not paying attention to any of the service. She looked at the stained glass windows and statues like a young child. When it came time for Communion, she followed Annie. She didn't stop her. Nayette needed all the help she could get, but they received more than one disapproving look.

After Mass they went for lunch. While they waited for their food, Nayette sheepishly admitted that she had broken the medicine pouch. Annie had to stifle the anger she felt. Not only had Nayete taken a spiritual gift, she had disrespected it. Annie looked at it carefully to quiet her emotions. On examination, it was clear that it was truly unique. It was made of carefully woven beads lined with fabric instead of the usual beaded hide. It was clear the beads were very old, and the threads were worn. It could have broken at any time.

"Would you fix it?" she asked.

Most of the beads were in the little sack she had put the pouch in, so Annie said she would try. It had been given to Nayette, and Annie couldn't disrespect the gift by refusing to restore it.

When they finished eating, Nayette said she wanted to go pray with the items Annie had brought. When they got in the car, she guided them out of town to a butte, known to the local tribe as the place where their stories originated. The isolated butte rose before them. A faint path wound to the flat, grassy top. Wind blowing from the north caused the grasses to wave in invitation. It was a very special place.

Annie had not been one to smudge others, her friend Mary was always the one who lit first the sage for cleansing, then the sweetgrass to bring spiritual blessing. She was awkward getting everything ready, first preparing the sage and lighting it, waiting for the smoke to rise. After they waved the smoke over their bodies, she lit the sweetgrass. It was difficult because the wind kept blowing out the matches. Nayette reverently washed the smoke first over her head, and then over the rest of her. They prayed together, and Nayette truly appreciated the little ceremony. When they got back to the facility, she asked if Annie would come again. Annie told her she would when she could. Annie was surprised when on the way home that she felt happy and fulfilled.

Annie was able to put the pouch back to near original using some of her own beads which nearly matched. She wasn't able to fix all the tiny holes worn in the ancient fabric.

Annie brought the medicine pouch to Nayette when she took her to make arrangements for money to go see her children. Annie was shocked when Nayette came out of her room. The shorts she wore were so tight and revealing the curve of her buttocks hung below the cuff. The top she wore barely covered her breasts. Annie begged her to change. Nayette insisted that if they didn't like her the way she was, it was their problem. Annie sighed in resignation as they went to the car.

They walked into the courthouse to stares of disgust. But those did not compare to the reception Nayette got from the woman who could have given her the OK to get money and tickets for travel. After looking Nayette up and down, she raised her head, looking down a nose searching for the source of putrid odor, lips down turned in scorn. Nayette vehemently pleaded, stating her right to her own money, which was in the control of her guardian. Annie tried to intercede, but it was clear that no argument would change the woman's mind. She refused to call Nayette's guardian, simply turning her back and ignoring Nayette's pleas. The forty mile drive home on a two lane grain truck rutted highway seemed endless.

They went to Mass again a few weeks later. It was to be the last time, since Annie and her husband were moving away. Nayette proudly wore the pouch. Her dress was more conservative, skirt and blouse that actually covered her discreetly. When the service was over, Nayette looked down at her blouse, her eyes widening. Patting herself down all over she looked at Annie helplessly.

"It's gone!" she said incredulously.

"What's gone?" Annie asked.

"I can't find the pouch! You saw it. I was wearing it and now it's gone!"

They searched all around where they had been sitting. She searched her pockets, and felt all over her body again.

"I can't find the pouch!"

She continued searching on the floor, her voice rising in panic.

"I can't find it!"

Annie helped her look, but the pouch was nowhere to be found.

"I will ask Father to watch for it. It's bound to show up."

After a few more minutes of searching without finding the pouch, Nayette grudgingly agreed to leave. The pouch wasn't in the parking lot or on the church steps. The loss frightened her. She really did have respect.

As usual, they went to the butte. They immediately searched the car, but the pouch wasn't there. It was a bit windy, but Annie had never had any real problem getting the sweet grass to burn before. But this time, it simply would not light. Annie tried inside the car, but that didn't work either. Nayette was getting more and more panicky.

"If the sweet grass won't light, that means I am going to die. It's because I lost the pouch!"

Nayette was inconsolable. Since each failure of lighting the sweetgrass made her more frantic, Annie took her back to town.

Parking in front of the building where Nayette was living, they prayed for the return of the pouch and the many needs they would never have another chance to pray about together. When she seemed calm enough, Annie went inside with her. Nayette gave Annie her first beadwork, a carefully done bead-wrapped key holder. Then we said our goodbyes. It was sad leaving her there in the confines of a home for the elderly.

On the drive home, Annie thought about her times with Nayette. She thought about how different people seem to be when you decide to be a part of their lives, and let them be a part of yours. She would miss Nayette. And she puzzled over the loss of the medicine pouch. Was she right in having fears of death? Nayette had shown a dark side when she tried to get Annie to cut off a lock of her hair so that her sister could curse someone for her. Still, she dismissed the dire prediction.

True to her word, Annie did contact the church a few times to see if the pouch turned up. It was never found. Four months after they moved, Annie got another call about Nayette. She had managed to sneak out of assisted living, and had gone on a drinking binge. She died as a result. Nayette was free at last.

THERESA

1992

When a child is killed, some parents stand and fight for justice, while others run away. Annie and Craig ran. They had seen the empty look on the faces of a couple whose son had been killed on the high school steps; had seen the cold, patronizing looks of the town's people. They ran, too, in self imposed oblivion. There had been no justice for the parents of the young man: their son was killed by the mayor's jealous son. If charges were filed, they were meaningless since the only punishment was two weeks in the state mental facility. He was never seen again, at least in town.

Annie and Craig knew the look. It was on the faces of the people in the emergency room when their daughter Theresa was killed. An accident, they were told. But the looks on the faces of the others who were snowmobiling with her told a different story. Some years later, a chance conversation with a plain clothes officer who investigated suspicious deaths explained the main detail that causes suspicion: sudden death of a primary witness. Theresa's husband had just such a friend: the town's soon to be married detective, out on his first snowmobile run. The friend who, a few weeks later, committed suicide.

"It's all right Mom, it's all right."

Those few words seemed to dissolve all the distance that had grown up between mother and daughter the last few years. Theresa held her mother's hand as she repeated the words. They cried together, tears of relief and love. Yet it couldn't be. Theresa was buried that morning.

The rift began when Theresa married Charlie - Charlie, who was considered responsible for her death. It was amazing how such a tragic end of life generated so many amazing events. It started with her Rosary. The service began with a few prayers and a short talk by her favorite priest. Then Theresa's nephew Jake played *Stairway to Heaven* on his guitar Theresa's sister Lydia gave a short, impassioned eulogy, and her brother Andy said a few tear filled words. Somewhere in that short time, a feeling came over the little chapel. A feeling of love, of power.

Father announced to the almost exclusively Protestant gathering that the Rosary would be prayed. He said that anyone who would rather not participate could leave. No one left.

In the front row were Theresa's parents Craig and Annie, with their son Steve and his wife Sandy. They were all holding hands as if being held together by some unseen presence. This presence was so strong that it seemed impossible for them to let go. Two women from the church, friends of Annie's, led the prayers. They were life-long Catholics who prayed the Rosary daily. Yet, not far into the Rosary, they started leaving out words, even whole prayers. They seemed to be holding each other up. When they were finished, Father announced that the service was finished:

"Go in peace to love and serve the Lord". No one left.Annie and Craig looked at each other.

"Maybe we are supposed to go first, since no one leaving".

So after a time, they got up and went to the casket, where their beautiful daughter lay. Her pale, porcelain smooth skin and thick dark hair were as perfect as in life. How could she be laying there so still, so permanently? Trembling, they said their goodbyes, and went out to the foyer. No one left.

Annie and Craig found a bench and sat, waiting for the others to come out. They held each other's hands, still feeling the presence of Love. After 20 minutes, they went to see if their family members were coming, or if they had left by the side door, since no one had come past them. When they looked into the chapel, everyone was still there. No one had left.

That night, Annie had the first of many dreams. She dreamed that she saw Theresa dressed in a filmy, long gown being escorted by a man with long braids wearing a buckskin outfit so new it had no beadwork, no decoration. She called to Theresa, yet her daughter didn't respond, but kept looking upward. Some time later, Annie disclosed her dream to her friend Christine. Christine's eyes widened, and she took a deep breath.

She said "I haven't told you this because I was afraid you'd think I'm crazy. I saw a man just like you described standing behind her casket. He was as tall as the vaulted ceiling, and his arms reached straight out, touching the walls of the side chapels. Then I saw Theresa, dressed in a filmy gown, rise out of her casket and go straight up through the top of the church. He is the same man who works on the other side of you when you have your eyes closed and I am giving you a massage. When you have asked me if I can reach that far I never answered you. Now you know."

Theresa came to Annie many times in dreams, and always Annie could feel Theresa's smooth, cool cheek against hers. Then the dream that was bound to come: Theresa came to visit Annie in a dream, wearing the black coat that made her look so elegant. Theresa was wearing her favorite perfume, and her makeup was flawless, as was her dark, curled hair. She was as beautiful as Annie remembered. They talked for awhile. Then Theresa said as she hugged her mother.

"I have to go." It was the last time.

GRAND COULEE

1991

Early morning mist hung over Flathead Lake as Lois gathered the last minute items she was taking on her trip with Annie: her son's tent, the red traditional dance dress Annie had made for her, and her hawk feather fan given to her by a friend. She hadn't left the rez except to go to college since she had come there as a bride some 35 years before. Anticipation won out over anxiety. She and Annie were going to the annual powwow at Nespelem.

"Oh, where did I put my shawl?" Ravages of diabetes had taken their toll with her memory. She had to have her shawl or she couldn't dance.

"There you are, you little rascal" she giggled, "right where I left you!" The green shawl, made of synthetic fibers, was a necessity if she planned to dance, She thought of the long fringe swishing against her body as she took the little lady steps to the rhythm of the drum. A shiver of anticipation went through her.

She hadn't been so close to her home and family since she was swept away by her Indian lover. Oh, he was so handsome! And she was so young. He fell in love with her laugh, she fell in love with running off with her prince to never - never land. Of course, it didn't end up that way. It seldom does.

She looked out the window for the umpteenth time. She was riding with her friend Annie, who ran the local crisis center. It was still early, barely light. But she was anxious to get on the road. It was a long drive from the Flathead to the Colville rez, six hours if they didn't stop. Lois would have driven herself, but since Annie had seen her weaving all over the East shore road one night, she wouldn't let her drive herself. She had lost an eye when a boy she was babysitting accidentally shot a toy in her eye, losing her depth perception.

Annie stopped in front of Lois' little '30's house. It sat back from the street, white with a red front door which showed just barely behind the screen. Lois had the blinds pulled down except for the one she kept looking out. It was raised just enough to peek out. Annie got out and opened the trunk, hoping everything would fit. Excitedly, the short woman nearly ran up the walkway to the front door which Lois threw open. They did their little dance, hugging and rocking. Annie was just as anxious as Lois to 'get on the road'.

"Lois, Lois, Lois – are you ready to rumble?" Annie joked.

"Yes, ma'am!" Lois saluted and smiled.

"OK. Let's get your things, and get out of Dodge!"

"What's this", Annie asked as Lois struggled with a large canvas carrier.

"My son loaned this tent to me since we were going so far. He thought it would be more comfortable than the little ones we usually bring to powwows on the rez. I didn't want to make him feel bad, so I took it. It will be nice to have one that isn't so cramped."

Lois was used to her boys fussing over her. Annie wished, ever so briefly, that her own children were that caring. The two struggled to carry Lois's tent. It was heavier than they had anticipated. Annie remembered Lois having a small pup tent she took with her to powwows. The weight of the larger tent was a surprise, and the two women struggled to get it into the trunk. Annie had already hung her teal dance outfit with her fuschia shawl on the hook behind the driver's seat along with her hawk feather fan. With a querying look, Lois asked where she should put her regalia. Annie indicated the hook behind the passenger's seat.

Lois was visibly anxious to be going off the rez, and so was

Annie. Annie was born in Wenatchee; her mother had gone to school in Omak, just on the edge of the Colville. Lois never talked about where she was born, but Annie heard it was in somewhere in Washington. Lois avoided any reference to her family. Perhaps because she had married an Indian, but Annie guessed it went deeper than that. It was a moot detail. But to leave the Flathead and go to where there was dancing and drumming – and after all these years!

Annie closed the full trunk with vigor, and they were on their way. She had gassed up the night before, they had snacks for the trip, and Lois had filled the thermos with fresh coffee: two somewhat plump middle-aged women off on an adventure, singing and giggling.

Leaving Flathead Lake behind, they drove up over the Flathead moraine and out on to prairie. Some 20 more miles, and the red and black Chevy Cavalier trudged up Ravalli Hill, winding down the steep Bison Range hillside then making the right hand swoop over the Jocko, toward the Flathead River which flowed over the dam north of town, winding it's way south. Few homes dotted the hillside along the winding, tree lined road. Following the Flathead for many miles, they took a left onto the serpentine road going toward St. Regis alongside the Clark Fork River. The deciduous trees which grew alongside the Flathead turned to pine forest in the tight canyon. The sweet smell of pine filled the air. There was little conversation; the women were lost in thoughts about the trip.

"Oh look! There is the campground where we had that Cursillo day of reflection," Lois happily recalled.

"Yes, that was a really special time" added Annie, "and the singing!" A smile played on her face.

Once they reached the interstate, they turned West toward Idaho, then on to Washington and the powwow. Up over the mountain passes and onto the flat. Everything was going smoothly, the atmosphere in the Cavalier was one of happy expectation.

Lois was anxious to stop at Grand Coulee Dam. She had

heard of a tour you could take down into the bowels of the dam. The two ate lunch under the trees since the under-dam trip was an hour away. It was a relief to get in the shade, since the weather had turned oppressively hot, and there was no wind to ameliorate the heat.

Electric City, well named. As they sat on the grass, Annie became aware of the low hum of electrical activity. You could even smell its presence, causing Annie to feel a bit unsettled. Lois looked at her watch. Just about time. She reached her hand to Annie with a nod toward the building where the tour started. Annie demurred, shaking her head.

"I'll wait here". She didn't like a confining area: it made her want to run, and she feared not being able to get free.

She decided to lie down and take a nap while Lois went on the touristy tour. Looking up through the umbrella of elm, she could see the clouds and the hot looking sky. Soon she became drowsy, and drifted off.

She jerked awake at Lois' touch. The short nap had refreshed her: the excitement, the driving, the heat and the food had worked to make her drowsy, but the nap had refreshed her. Lois giggled as Annie struggled to get to her feet. "Getting Old?" she quipped.

"Yeah, right!"Annie playfully smarted back.

They gathered their leftovers and went to the car. They went across the face of the dam, and turned left toward Nespelem, and the powwow. Annie was suddenly anxious. She started to shake.

"Lois, I'm going to have to pull over. I don't know what is happening to me." Just ahead a pullout was on the river side of road. Annie stopped the little Chevy and got out.

"Oh, my! I haven't been here since I was a three-year-old. My Uncle Ray and Aunt Lucy brought me here when the dam was under construction. I have dreamed it over and over: the same feelings I just started to have back then. Shaking, restricted breathing, tight stomach. To have it become so strong is strange;

I wasn't even thinking about it." They stayed at the turnout for a few minutes until Annie calmed down. Then they went on the few miles to the powwow.

When they got to Nespelem, they easily found the powwow grounds. There were a few teepees up already, their white canvas walls gleaming in the sun, the flags at the top of the poles fluttering in the light breeze. A man at the entrance handed them programs and asked if they were planning on staying overnight, then indicated where they could set up their tent: on the right, outside the low fence where only teepees were allowed. The dance arbor was ready and a few venders were already set up.

They picked a spot across the road from the arbor to put up their tent. It was quite a project to get all the stakes into the solid ground. So once they got their sleeping bags inside, they decided to take a look around at the venders, then to sit on the bleachers under the arbor. There were very few dancers, and they felt a bit uncomfortable. They got stares: "two white women at a powwow who don't belong", the looks seemed to say

"Let's go lie down. Then when it's dark and there are more people, we can come back," Lois opined.

"Sounds good", Annie responded.

So, the two lay down on their respective bags. Lois fell asleep quickly. She had lost the sight and hearing on one side, so she lay on her good side. Annie fell asleep soon after, waking up after dark to the sound of young voices outside. They sounded as if they had been drinking or were on drugs. Whispering and giggling. She decided to listen more carefully, then wishing she hadn't. She didn't know what to do. It was clear that Lois and Annie were the topic of their quietly conspiratorial conversation.

"Let's kill the old white ladies".

Giggles.

"OK!"

Annie froze. She wasn't sure what to do. She waited until the voices had moved on. Were they joking? It didn't sound like it.

Even if they were just kidding... but what if they weren't? She didn't want to wake Lois in case they were still waiting out there. She ended up falling back to sleep. When she woke again it was completely dark outside.

She quietly got out of the tent. She must have been sleeping hard. There were tents and vehicles all around. The air was heavy with smoldering sage. A drum group sang a familiar song, the driving sound carrying heavily through the night. She looked at the area away from the arbor. There was room to drive there, but there didn't appear to be a way to get back out onto the road. She knew she had to try. Carefully getting into the car, she closed the door gently, leaving Lois to sleep.

Heart pounding, shaking, she kept driving, dodging the other campsites. The ground was uneven, causing the car to bounce around precipitously. There was no movement around the camps. Campfires were banked. Everyone was either sleeping or at the powwow. Finally when she got to a spot where the camps were not so close together; she maneuvered the car to get through to the road. It had taken her to the other side of the powwow grounds. There was a large crowd of people in dance outfits, and some in street clothes. Drumming and singing. How had she been able to sleep so long with the intrusive sounds? She recalled praying that God would let her sleep till the young people were gone, but this late?

By the time she got to the road, she could see men's fancy dancers on the sawdust dance ground, whirling and stomping under the arbor, and the drumming and singing were almost deafening. Annie saw any number of young people talking and laughing. Were they the ones who had threatened their lives? She didn't know what they looked like. Her heart hadn't settled down. Is this how all the women who came to her felt when they were threatened by their husbands or boyfriends? Terrified, she kept driving around the grounds until she got to the place closest to the tent. Getting out of the car and leaving the door ajar, she went to the tent and touched Lois on the shoulder.

"Lois. We have to go. Get your things, we have to go."

Lois got up without a word, carrying her suitcase out to the car, and never asked why. When they got to the car, Annie explained why she had insisted on leaving. Still shaking, she drove around the circle to get back out and on through the little town and out on to the highway. The closest town was about forty miles away, the first town off the rez. The night was moonless, and the road wound around and around. Every car seemed to hold a threat. They 'weren't in Kansas anymore'!

Annie always felt safe on the Flathead Reservation, but this was strange territory. Lois had lived on the lake ever since her wedding. Annie had only lived there for a few years. Each woman, lost in thought, spoke little beyond where they were going, where they would sleep. Nothing about what might have happened.

Omak was off the reservation, just on the other side of the Okanogan River. It was very late, the town was asleep. They finally found a motel but it had all its lights off. Annie banged on the door until a sleepy woman with her hair up in curlers and wearing a robe answered, saying they were closed. She must have sensed their urgency, since she relented and took them to a room.

They knew they needed to go back to get the tent. If it hadn't belonged to Lois' son, they could have just left it at the powwow grounds. It was the only thing they discussed, each lost in her own thoughts. Were they foolish for running away? What if they had stayed? The next morning, after a restless night, they went to breakfast in Omak. In the light of day, the terror of the night before seemed to disappear.

They drove back over the bridge and onto the reservation, back to the place where, it had seemed, danger was present. The road didn't seem as threatening in the light of day. They even stopped at the Chief Joseph Memorial on the outskirts of Nespelem. The women joked about how silly they were to think that they were targeted by young kids. They entered the road that they had left so quickly the night before. Getting out of the car, they walked to the canvas tent. No one paid attention to them, they were all across the road at the powwow, or wandering through the vendors' stands, fry bread in hand. Everything appeared to be normal,.until they got close.

All of the tent stakes except for the four corners were removed and were lying on the ground. Lois looked at her friend as if to say 'you saved our lives'. When they went into the tent, they found that water had been thrown onto the floor, the sleeping bags were soaked. And in the middle of the floor, a crowbar.

They took the sleeping bags out and removed the remaining four stakes from the ground, folding the tent as quickly as they could, just enough to put it in the trunk of the car. They left as quickly as they could, looking around cautiously. Everyone was across the road at the festivities.

It was only after they were on the road that they talked, even laughed a little. It was probably only a prank. When they got back to the Flathead Reservation, Lois told an elder about their experience. He looked at her and said "Yes, they would have killed you. You are lucky that your friend was alert and got you out of there."

The next Thursday morning, when the women met with their friends for coffee and to visit, Lois told the story of their adventure. Her eyes filled with tears as she thanked God for alerting them to the danger, for Annie's concern, and her own willingness to go when she was asked.

THE LETTER

2003

Annie looked out the window toward the soaring mountains. Glancing up at the ancient ponderosa that framed the majestic Rockies, she watched as fresh snowflakes drifted to the ground. Much as she treasured the last snow of winter that gave the promise of spring, it meant that her son would postpone his trip from North Dakota. It was blizzarding there, and the trip would be dangerous. He would be tired from working long hours on the oil rigs. Disappointed that the weather had changed, Annie decided to find a project to keep her mind occupied. Turning away from the window, a dull light spot on a drawer of the dark oak china secretary caught her attention. Apparently someone had used a commercial wood cleaner on it causing the wood on one of the drawers to look dry and bleached.

The china secretary also known as the 'cluge' after an engineering slang term, was treasured not only by her, but by her grandchildren as well. The curved glass door allowed little ones to see the tantalizing treasures on the five narrow shelves. They were allowed to see, but not touch the delicate old objects. By a certain age, when only one child was around, she would take them out one at a time for a closer look, but no touching. A little rite of passage. When one of them got to an age to be trusted, and schooled in careful handling, they were given the honor of holding the objects. There were the mother of pearl opera glasses, over one hundred years old, and the dainty little china vase treasured by her mother.

It was special not only for its age, over one hundred years, but mostly because of how she came to have it. Looking through a familiar old barn full of antiques, she had come across a tall dark oak piece she had never seen before. A bowed glass door and three matching bowed drawers below a slanted drop down door with raised scrolling, it was topped by a beveled mirror finished off with more scrolling. Standing in front of it she looked up and saw her face in the mirror. Nothing of note for most, but to 4'9" Annie, it was amazing. She thought about it for days, dreamed of it sometimes at night. Finally she told her husband Craig about it. Seeing how much it meant to her, Craig bought it for her, selling his Martin classical guitar to get the money to buy it. She treasured it more because of his sacrifice.

An expert in the care of antique furniture recommended using a combination of turpentine and beeswax to care for the wood. Annie got out the smelly concoction and applied a little to the drawer front. She rubbed away some of her disappointment in caring for something so special to her. She pulled out the drawer a few inches to wax the top rim. She paused after a few rubs. This was one of her memory drawers, filled with old pictures her children had drawn, report cards, athletic schedules and old letters.

Memories.

She took the drawer out and sat it on a chair, carefully removing the papers one at a time. Some were over fifty years old and delicate. Handling each piece of her children's memorabilia served to take her back in time. Most of it was pleasant, heartwarming. Then she found an envelope full of her junior high report cards. She discovered her grades were not as wonderful as she remembered. Finally, she looked at the letters. Annie read the one from an aunt whose husband had recently died and her struggle with missing her one true love. Several were from old neighbors.

The last was from her mother, sent years ago after her mother's surgery for cancer. Annie didn't want to read it. Just handling it reminded her of the many times she had felt put down, ignored, and treated unfairly. Things like incinerating her artwork portfolio, keeping Annie from entering an art institute with portfolio requirements. The times when her mother would leave a store or a parking lot if she saw her after Annie joined the Catholic Church, a church she didn't understand or approve. Annie put the letter aside. No use spoiling the day she had just managed to make better regardless of her disappointment over the housekeeper's mistake.

Annie left the drawer on a chair and went to get some lunch. The letter from her mother sat on top of the pile, but was not forgotten. She sat where she could see up into the mountains. She could relate to the Natives who called the rugged peaks their mother. It was comforting, keeping that relationship distant, impersonal.

Putting her plate with a half eaten sandwich aside, Annie went back to the task at hand: replacing the drawer with the unread letter on top. She somehow felt she should read it, steeling herself against any criticism. It wasn't in an envelope. She slowly unfolded it. There was a row of spring flowers in orange and lavender across the top of the single pale yellow page. The date was July 24, 1985. .

Annie remembered the trip – hour after hour on the train to Southern California, wondering how her mother's surgery would turn out, how her teenage kids would behave in her absence, how she would feel if........she didn't want to deal with the 'if's". Instead, she wrote a poem expressing her faith in God's healing power.

Annie's eyes focused on the words in her mother's hand: 'My Dear Annie", it began. After the usual formalities it went on, "I want you to know how much it meant to me having you here with me, how when you prayed with me Jesus became real to me. It comes back when I think of you."

Tears blurred the rest of the words. After awhile, Annie folded the short letter and carefully placed it on the top of the contents of the drawer and slowly slipped it back in place. Her mother had recovered: all the cancer was removed. Again she lifted her eyes to the mountains, thinking about the letter and its importance. People can change. They can be touched by others. Hurt can be healed – we need to listen and accept that healing and the love of others.

Annie picked up the cloth soaked with beeswax and turpentine and put another coat on the drawer. As she buffed it back to a deep dark brown, she thought long and hard about the letter, about letting go of old hurts, and concentrating on the love of a mother for her child. Her mother's for her child: Annie's love for her own children.

Into The Circle

2001

As Annie walked up the street to go for lunch, she heard the pounding of drums. At first, she thought it was a car radio, but as Annie got closer, she saw the back of a pickup with a drum and several young Native American men sitting around it, shining black braids flying as they pounded out the rhythm to their chant-like song. This impromptu street powwow was just one of the amazing things Annie experienced in the short time she had been on the reservation.

Getting closer, Annie held at the back of the crowd watching the moves of the dancers, feeling the drum throb in her chest, completely absorbed in the experience. A slight touch on her shoulder, and the words "You belong in the circle", took Annie by surprise. Turning toward the soft voice, she looked into eyes of such depth and beauty that the words didn't sink in. Their clear golden brown seemed to see things no one else could see.

"You belong in the circle", she repeated. She looked at Annie more closely. "You're not *from* here. Come."

The drum and singers started what Annie came to know as a round, or friendship dance. Dancers form a circle and step to one side in rhythm to the drum. Her new friend pulled Annie gently but firmly into the circle of dancers. Stumbling around the circle, she couldn't seem to make her feet do the right moves.

Getting over her self-absorbed embarrassment, Annie's attention turned toward this beautiful woman. Her fine brown hair was caught back with a tie, golden highlights matching the gold in her eyes. She wasn't much taller than Annie, making her around five feet, slim of face and body. She reminded Annie of her favorite movie star.

The little powwow broke up, since lunchtime was over, and the drummers and main dancer had to get back to work. That was the only time that a powwow was out on the street while Annie lived there. This lady was to appear unexpectedly many times in her life. Brianna, as she came to know her, would become an important part of Annie's life. Over the years, a small, tentative voice on the phone would say "Annie?", and she would know immediately it was Brianna. Sometimes she would ask how to handle a troublesome person, but mostly it was as a respectful friend. It was not unusual for her to have a bit of wisdom to share.

Annie came to know Brianna's daughter Stephanie, who had been molested. Social Services sent her to Annie's office to work with her. Annie gathered a couple of girls who had similar experiences and showed them a prevention film to facilitate conversation. At the end of the film, Stephanie put her chin on her cupped hand, looked the other girls in the eye, and said, "Well, who molested you?"

All Annie had to do was to watch and ask an occasional question. The girls ran the show.

Brianna came to the office ostensibly to say how much better her daughter was doing. After niceties, she began to reveal her past, how she had experienced trauma in her early years. Then she revealed that recently she had been robbed by an acquaintance and then raped. It was bad enough that she had the frightening and demeaning experience, but when she went to court, the perpetrator got several years for the robbery, no time for the rape.

As with many young Native women, Brianna had used alcohol and drugs to cope with the poverty and violence that often exists on reservations. Things really went down hill for her after the break-in and attack. Left with fewer resources and lowered self-esteem, Social Services saw fit to take custody of her children. Devastated, she found coming to the office helpful. As an advocate Annie was able to connect her with resources that led to getting adequate housing and other vital services, requisite for reuniting with her children. After a year or so, she was able to get them back. Annie hadn't seen anyone fight as hard as Brianna did to bring her children home.

Brianna told Annie that she helped her get her children back from Social Services. This is common for women who have been victimized; anything good that happens in their lives must be the result of someone else's effort, not theirs. Annie may have guided Brianna to resources or helped her phrase things in a way that got the powers that be to listen, but it was always her own effort, her own determination to get her children back, that made it happen.

Soon after Annie moved to the reservation, she had the opportunity to make a coed Cursillo weekend. For her, it was three days of rollercoaster emotions, but in the end, she learned that men can be just as touched by God as women, and that there really is such a thing as Christian community. This may seem obvious, but it had not been part of her experience.

Annie lost touch with Brianna, and hadn't seen her for about a year before she decided to move back to her husband and grown family. It had been a fruitful three years, and knew she would miss her new friends, especially her Native American friends.

She and her husband came to the reservation every year to look for a place to buy a little land to build a house. He, too, had made a Cursillo weekend, and felt the powerful pull of the People. He would laugh at Annie, because everywhere they went, she would look for Brianna. In markets, she would be disappointed because Annie thought that surely she would find Brianna at the end of the next aisle. They came to the reservation a couple of times a year, and always searched the crowd for her. But it didn't happen.

They finally moved to the reservation, and attended the Catholic mission church. Soon after the move, they were at Mass, and the church was very full. At the sign of peace, Annie looked around her as they all shook hands. Over on the far side of the church, Annie thought she saw a familiar face. With people moving around, she couldn't be sure, but it looked like Brianna! All through the rest of Mass Annie kept twisting and turning to get a better look. It had to be her. Annie's husband asked her what her problem was and she nearly blurted aloud "I think its Brianna!" By then he was so familiar with her search, he knew who Annie was talking about. She looked one more time, and with tears in her eyes,

"It's her!"

He told Annie "Go over to the other side of the church as close as you can, so that you won't miss her!"

So right in the middle of Communion prayers, Annie made her way to the pews closest to where Brianna was. When Mass ended, Brianna turned to leave and saw Annie. Brianna was just as thrilled as Annie was. They hugged and danced around, cried, and made a lot of noise.

"It's you! It's really you!" they both cried. People all around smiled and laughed, joining in their happy reunion.

Brianna lived about thirty miles from the couple, but husband and wife made the trip about once a month. She lived in a variety of marginal apartments and houses, wherever she could get cheap rent. In one, her son Kenny was sleeping on the floor next to a moldy wall. They took a twin bed used for company to him so he could get off the floor. Years later, when her husband had a huge tumor removed from his chest, Kenny went to the sweat lodge to pray for him three days in a row. Annie's husband never took a pain pill, and healed much faster than expected.

Brianna would come to their home when Annie was able to go get her. They would walk the dusty road at the edge of the forest, and she would point out the use for various plants. When Annie asked who taught her, she would reply that she just knew. And

Annie believed her. She would talk of her Brother Jesus on their walks, but always pointed out that the cross was terrifying to her. She had been told frightening stories as a child and never got over it. She had been baptized a Catholic as an infant, but her family seldom went to Mass. She held on to many of her tribe's ancient traditions, but she didn't share those. She did say that she would like to sweat, but didn't trust those who had invited her. There were rumors of sweat lodge ceremonies that called on bad forces.

When a Cursillo weekend was in the planning at their parish, Annie and her husband discussed asking her if she would like to go. They did, and she agreed. She was a little nervous to be away from her children for three full days, especially in a church setting with many non-Indians. The couple prayed all weekend for her and sent encouraging notes. When they took her home, she was really amazed at what a wonderful, spiritual weekend she had experienced. Shortly after they picked her up to take her home, she gave each one an eagle feather.

Her son Ken became close with Annie's husband, giving him symbolic drawings of buffalo and braves. Because of Brianna's poverty, they obviously never expected any material things from her. One day she called and asked to come and visit, something she seldom did, waiting to be asked. When they got settled on their little deck, she said that she had a dream about Annie that she was supposed to give her something. She brought out of her bag a beautifully made hand drum. She said Annie was supposed to use it 'for the children', and that she was to place a specific design on it to represent her and her family.

She honored them with several beaded pieces she had made specifically for them. Among them, a beautiful a wallet for Annie's husband and Rosaries she beaded for each of them. A turtle she beaded for Annie is on the handle of her powwow feather fan. She helped Annie buy fabric to make a powwow dress, making sure she knew the proper style and length, very concerned that Annie follow tradition.

After twenty years, they remain friends. Brianna has suffered from emotional problems all her life because of abuse. Her physical health has never been strong, and she had to quit working a few years ago. Tribal health made the judgment that her spiritual experiences are a result of mental illness, and she has been required to stay on medications. She does go through periods of depression and fear, flashbacks from early trauma. She hates the way they make her feel, and how the drugs block her connection with Creator and her Brother Jesus. At those times, she calls, and they talk until she gets back her self-esteem. It seems to help her to talk to Annie. They were recently talking about the medicine – or gifts – that people have. Annie said she doesn't have one.

Brianna sounded a little surprised. "Why, it's your voice. That's why I gave you the drum, to add its voice to yours."

She is Annie's wounded, healing friend, and she is grateful to know Brianna and her courage. Annie told her friend that she will continue to give Brianna the gift of her voice.

Strength in Weakness

"It's only for a checkup", Mother said.
Before long Annie was laying on a cold marble slab,
Ex-ray beds are different now.
Then she was put on a cart and wheeled away.
"Where was my mother? Shouldn't I be going home?"
"Look at this wall", the nurse said, pointing
to a huge glass case with lethal-looking weapons.
"These are the tools we are going to use on you today."
A man in a white coat with no face said,
"Count backward from 100" Annie got to 98.
She was only six.

Annie woke up in a crib with metal bars
alone in the middle of a bare room.
She could hear the laughter of children nearby.
Why was she alone?
"Oh, my dear, your heart surgery was a failure.
Their very first one," the nurse said almost proudly.
"Now don't sit up or move around.
If you need something, you just call."
Annie could hear buzzers going off down the hall,
And each time one sounded, a nurse came running.
Where was my buzzer? Annie really needed to go.
No buzzer. She really meant it. "Call".

Seldom did anyone come when Annie called.
She often woke up lying in wet sheets.
The night nurses complained,
"Why can't you use the bedpan?"
She would have if someone had brought one.
The days were long and lonely.
Where was my mother? Annie cried. A lot.

More days went by. The young voices quieted.
The night nurse with long painted nails
Told Annie they were all better and had gone home.
"When will I go home?"
"Now don't you worry!"
"When will my mother come?"
"On Saturdays"

Mother did come for a little while on Saturdays.
"Why didn't her operation work?" Mother once asked.
"Oh, it did the first few days.
But she cried so much she ruined it."
Mother didn't question her. But in her mind, Annie did.

Annie didn't believe anyone much after that,
But questioned everything,
even the teacher who tried to tell her
a squiggle on the board was a two.
"How do *you* know?"
If her very own mother would lie to her,
How could she trust anyone?
In school, Annie got strong.
Not in body, but surely in mind.
she got straight A's, and she didn't cry.
In weakness,
You can learn strength."

www.ingramcontent.com/pod-product-compliance
Ingram Content Group UK Ltd.
Pitfield, Milton Keynes, MK11 3LW, UK
UKHW020241250726
13967UKWH00001B/491

9 781304 424594